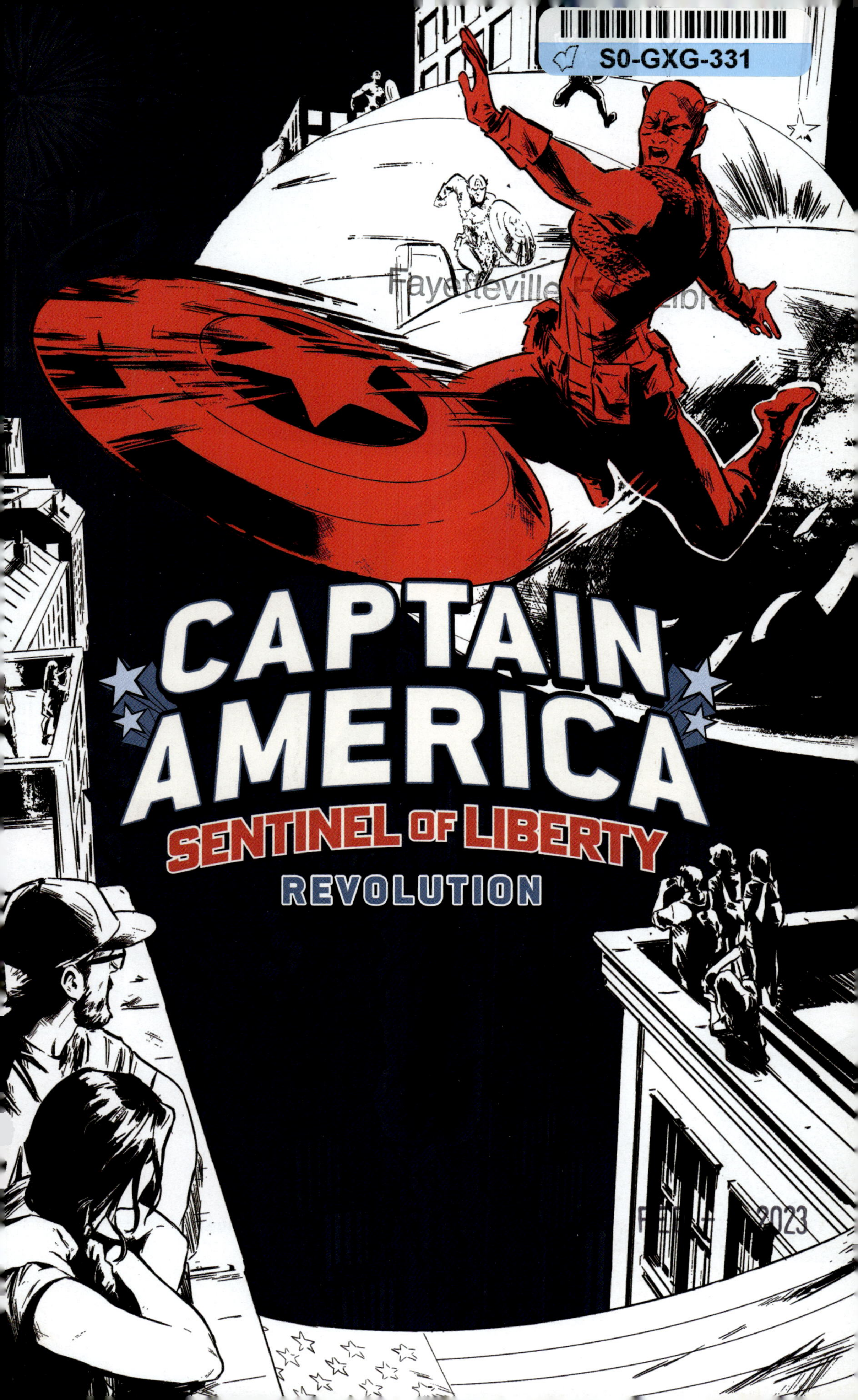
CAPTAIN AMERICA
SENTINEL OF LIBERTY
REVOLUTION

1940! As the world teetered on the brink of global war, frail Steve Rogers entered a secret laboratory and was transformed into the American Super-Soldier! For five thrilling years, he fought the Axis Powers — until a freak stroke of fate threw him into suspended animation. When he awoke, he was a man decades out of his time! Since that fateful day, Steve Rogers has sought his destiny in this brave new world!

LETTERER
VC's JOE CARAMAGNA

ASSISTANT EDITOR
KAITLYN LINDTVEDT

EDITOR
ALANNA SMITH

EXCUTIVE EDITOR
TOM BREVOORT

SPECIAL THANKS TO
PALOMA JOGA

COLLECTION EDITOR
DANIEL KIRCHHOFFER

ASSISTANT MANAGING EDITOR
MAIA LOY

ASSOCIATE MANAGER, TALENT RELATIONS
LISA MONTALBANO

DIRECTOR, PRODUCTION & SPECIAL PROJECTS
JENNIFER GRÜNWALD

VP PRODUCTION & SPECIAL PROJECTS
JEFF YOUNGQUIST

BOOK DESIGNERS
STACIE ZUCKER & CARLOS LAO

SENIOR DESIGNER
ADAM DEL RE

SVP PRINT, SALES & MARKETING
DAVID GABRIEL

EDITOR IN CHIEF
C.B. CEBULSKI

CAPTAIN AMERICA
SENTINEL OF LIBERTY
REVOLUTION

WRITERS
JACKSON LANZING & COLLIN KELLY

ARTIST
CARMEN CARNERO

COLOR ARTIST
NOLAN WOODARD

COVER ART
CARMEN CARNERO & ALEJANDRO SÁNCHEZ

CAPTAIN AMERICA #0

WRITERS
TOCHI ONYEBUCHI, JACKSON LANZING & COLLIN KELLY

ARTIST
MATTIA DE IULIS

COVER ART
ALEX ROSS

[C]APTAIN AMERICA CREATED BY JOE SIMON & JACK KIRBY

[CA]PTAIN AMERICA: SENTINEL OF LIBERTY VOL. 1 — REVOLUTION. Contains material originally published in magazine form as CAPTAIN AMERICA (2022) #0 and CAPTAIN AMERICA: SENTINEL OF LIBERTY (2022) #1-6. [Fir]st printing 2022. ISBN 978-1-302-93143-8. Published by MARVEL WORLDWIDE, INC., a subsidiary of MARVEL ENTERTAINMENT, LLC. OFFICE OF PUBLICATION: 1290 Avenue of the Americas, New York, NY 10104. © [20]22 MARVEL No similarity between any of the names, characters, persons, and/or institutions in this book with those of any living or dead person or institution is intended, and any such similarity which may exist is purely [co]incidental. **Printed in the U.S.A.** KEVIN FEIGE, Chief Creative Officer; DAN BUCKLEY, President, Marvel Entertainment; DAVID BOGART, Associate Publisher & SVP of Talent Affairs; TOM BREVOORT, VP, Executive Editor; NICK [LO]WE, Executive Editor, VP of Content, Digital Publishing; DAVID GABRIEL, VP of Print & Digital Publishing; SVEN LARSEN, VP of Licensed Publishing; MARK ANNUNZIATO, VP of Planning & Forecasting; JEFF YOUNGQUIST, [VP] of Production & Special Projects; ALEX MORALES, Director of Publishing Operations; DAN EDINGTON, Director of Editorial Operations; RICKEY PURDIN, Director of Talent Relations; JENNIFER GRÜNWALD, Director of [Pro]duction & Special Projects; SUSAN CRESPI, Production Manager; STAN LEE, Chairman Emeritus. For information regarding advertising in Marvel Comics or on Marvel.com, please contact Vit DeBellis, Custom Solutions & [Int]egrated Advertising Manager, at vdebellis@marvel.com. For Marvel subscription inquiries, please call 888-511-5480. **Manufactured between 11/25/2022 and 12/27/2022 by SEAWAY PRINTING, GREEN BAY, WI, USA.**

987654321

CAPTAIN AMERICA #0

WRETCHED INHABITANTS OF NEW YORK CITY!
TOO LONG HAVE YOU SUFFERED UNDER THE BINDING YOKE OF HUMAN CIVILIZATION-- AND SO I, ARNIM ZOLA, THE BIO-FANATIC, HAVE DESIGNED FOR YOU AN EXIT STRATEGY!
BEHOLD: THE ZOLAZOIC ROCKET! SEE AS IT SHEDS ITS CAPITALIST FACADE AND ASCENDS TO THE HEAVENS!
THERE, THE SUN'S RAYS SHALL ACTIVATE MY HYPEREVOLUTION COMPOUND, EVOLVING YOUR FRAIL HUMAN BODIES INTO A WORLD OF PERFECTED ZOLASAURUSES!
AND ALL I HAD TO DO WAS HIDE MY FACE AND MY NAME BEHIND SHELL COMPANIES! I HAVE ENDED YOUR WORLD, YOU SQUALID AMERICANS, AND I HAVE DONE IT WITHOUT BREAKING ANY OF YOUR CHILDISH "LAWS"!
NONE REMAIN WHO WOULD EVEN DEIGN TO DEFEND THE SANCTITY OF YOUR DISGUSTING AMERICA! NOW IS THE TIME FOR THE UNITED STATES OF Z--
OH, COME THE #$%& ON.

KLANG
KLANG
KLANG
KLANG
KLANG
KLANG
EVER GET TIRED OF THAT SOUND, STEVE?
ABSOLUTELY NOT, SAM.
LET FREEDOM RING.
DAMN RIGHT.
NICE SHIELD, BY THE WAY.
THANKS, YOU TOO. OBVIOUSLY.
SHE'S GOT SOME YEARS ON HER, BUT EVERYONE LOVES A CLASSIC.
SPEAKING OF CLASSIC: YOUR OLD FRIEND WITH THE TV FACE IS ABOUT TO RIP A HOLE IN NEW YORK CITY.
LET'S MAKE SURE THIS INTERSECTION'S THE ONLY THING ZOLA DESTROYS TODAY. YOU GO HIGH, I GO LOW?
SEE YOU ON THE OTHER SIDE, CAP.
YOU KNOW IT, CAP.

ROCKET'S NO GOOD WITHOUT ENGINES.
LET'S SEE WHAT WE CAN DO ABOUT THOSE.
WANG!

BOOM!
ROCKETS.
I DON'T HATE A LOT OF THINGS IN THIS WORLD...
...BUT I SURE DO HATE ROCKETS.
DID YOU THINK THIS WOULD BE THAT EASY, HERR ROGERS?
BZK!
NO, ZOLA.
I KNOW IT WILL BE.

ALL RIGHT. WE GOT A ROCKET. ROCKET'S GOT A PAYLOAD.
PAYLOAD HITS THE SUN, THE HYPER-THING GOES BOOM.
HYPER-THING GOES BOOM, WE ALL TURN INTO DINOSAURS.
DISABLE THE PAYLOAD, NO DINOSAURS.

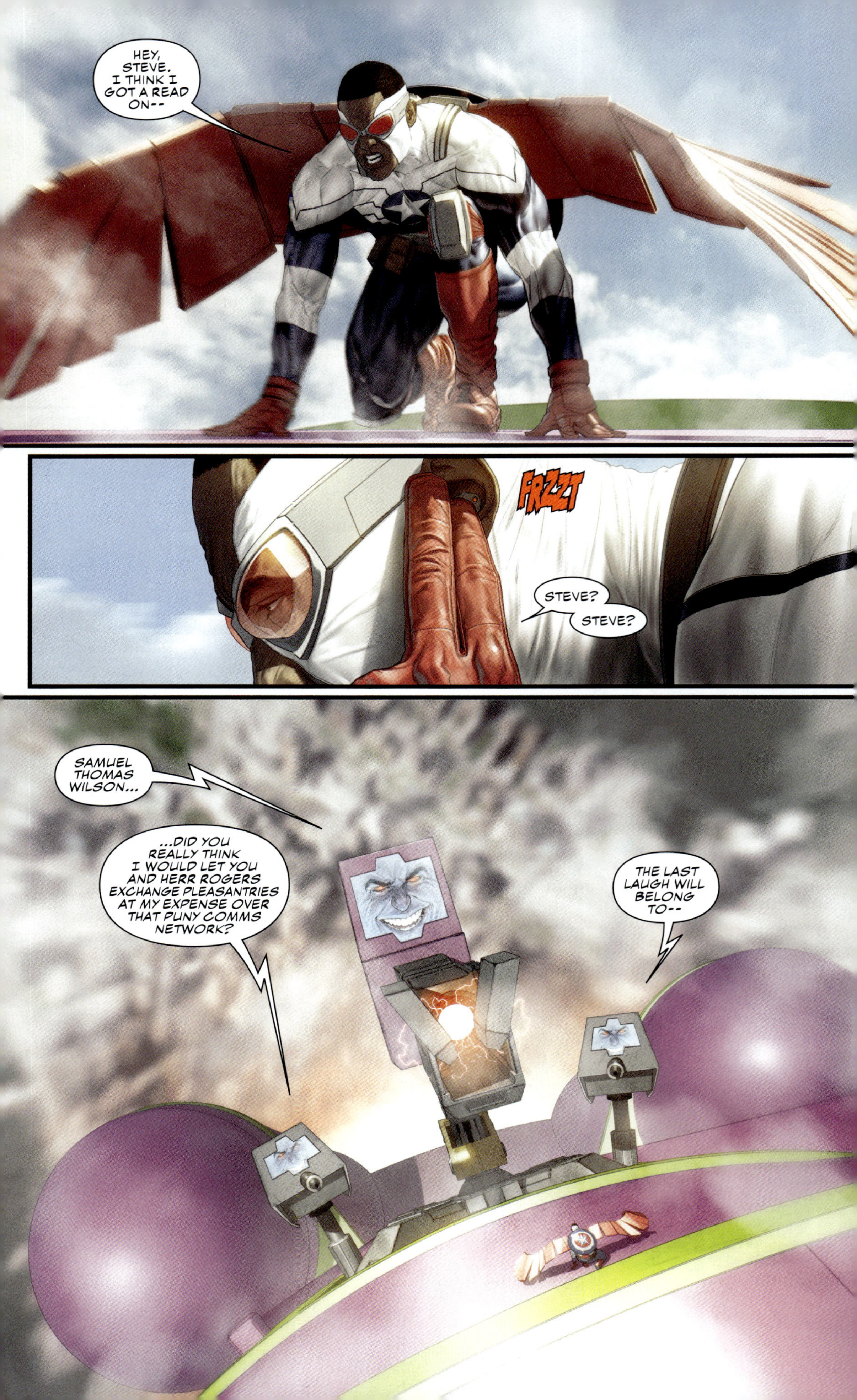
HEY, STEVE. I THINK I GOT A READ ON--
FRZZT
STEVE?
STEVE?
SAMUEL THOMAS WILSON...
...DID YOU REALLY THINK I WOULD LET YOU AND HERR ROGERS EXCHANGE PLEASANTRIES AT MY EXPENSE OVER THAT PUNY COMMS NETWORK?
THE LAST LAUGH WILL BELONG TO--

--ARNIM ZOLA! SAVIOR OF THE DYING WORLD!
WHY DO YOU INSIST ON ONCE AGAIN STANDING IN MY WAY?!
THIS WORLD ONLY NEEDS ONE THING FROM YOU, ZOLA...
CRUNCH!
...TO LEAVE YOU BEHIND!
RRRIIIP!
OKAY, SO MUCH FOR CUTTING THE ENGINES. CAN'T HAVE THIS FALLING ON THE CITY.
GUESS WE'RE GOING FOR CONTROL.

YES. CONTROL.
YOU'VE BECOME SO USED TO IT, HAVEN'T YOU, CAPTAIN?
IT TAKES A BOLD VISIONARY TO BREAK IT! TO DO WHAT MUST BE DONE FOR THE TRUE LIBERATION OF THIS WORLD!
THIS WORLD DOESN'T BELONG TO YOU, ZOLA.

NO. IT BELONGS TO THEM.
BUT I, ZOLA, THE SENTINEL OF LIBERTY, STRIKE BACK AGAINST THIS TERRIBLE DESTINY!
NOW WE SHALL WRITE A NEW THESIS! NOT ONE OF HUMANITY'S SURVIVAL, BUT OF OUR EVOLUTION!
AND WHAT MAKES YOU THINK THIS WILL BE THE ONE TIME I DON'T STOP YOU?
BECAUSE YOU ARE TRAPPED IN A ROCKET THAT IS GOING TO EXPLODE.
NOT MY FIRST TIME.

KNOCK, KNOCK.
NAME'S CAPTAIN AMERICA, BY THE WAY.
FIRE!
CAPTAIN AMERICA? WHAT AMERICA?

THE SAME AMERICA THAT WILL BE UNDERWATER IN LESS THAN TWO DECADES?
THE SAME AMERICA RAVAGED BY FIRES YOUR KIND ARE TOO PETTY TO ADDRESS?
THE SAME AMERICA THAT WOULD RATHER JAIL ITS OWN THAN COME TO TERMS WITH ITS ENVIRONMENT? THAT WOULD RAZE FORESTS TO BUILD PRISONS?
THAT AMERICA?

KSSSH
KRK
BZZT
KACHOOOOOOOOOOM!
YUP. THAT AMERICA.

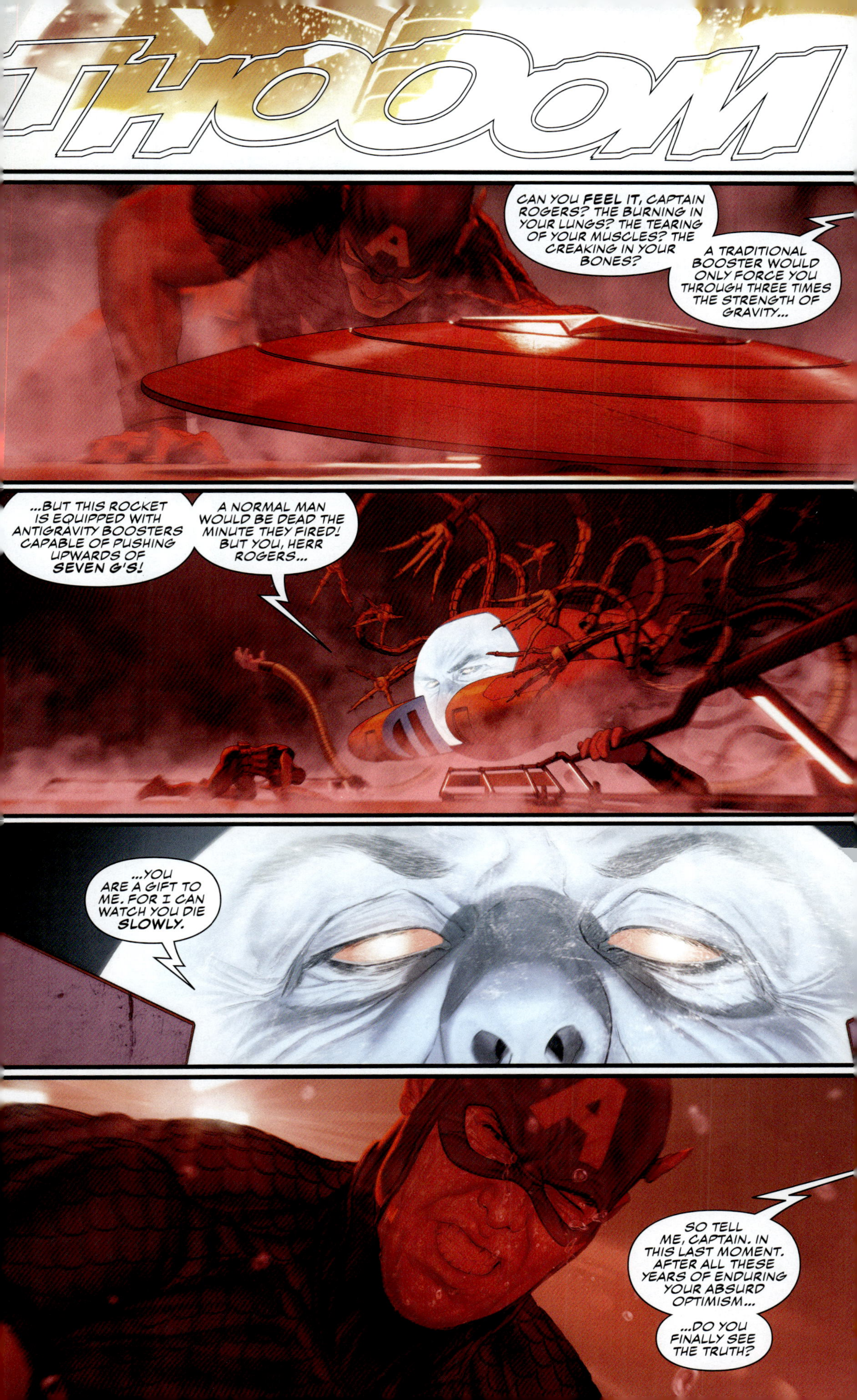
THOOOM
CAN YOU FEEL IT, CAPTAIN ROGERS? THE BURNING IN YOUR LUNGS? THE TEARING OF YOUR MUSCLES? THE CREAKING IN YOUR BONES?
A TRADITIONAL BOOSTER WOULD ONLY FORCE YOU THROUGH THREE TIMES THE STRENGTH OF GRAVITY...
...BUT THIS ROCKET IS EQUIPPED WITH ANTIGRAVITY BOOSTERS CAPABLE OF PUSHING UPWARDS OF SEVEN G'S!
A NORMAL MAN WOULD BE DEAD THE MINUTE THEY FIRED! BUT YOU, HERR ROGERS...
...YOU ARE A GIFT TO ME. FOR I CAN WATCH YOU DIE SLOWLY.
SO TELL ME, CAPTAIN. IN THIS LAST MOMENT. AFTER ALL THESE YEARS OF ENDURING YOUR ABSURD OPTIMISM...
...DO YOU FINALLY SEE THE TRUTH?

DO YOU SEE HOW CONTROLLED YOU ARE BY THE MILITARY THAT BUILT YOU? FROM YOUR HEAD TO YOUR HEART?
HOW THE ONLY ONES WHO TRULY BELIEVE AS YOU DO ARE OTHER FOSSILS OF A MORE IGNORANT TIME?
DO YOU HEAR NOW THE LIES YOU WERE FED BY THOSE YOU TRUSTED, EVEN IN YOUR GLORY DAYS?
DO YOU SEE HOW AMERICA HAS LEFT YOU BEHIND?
ALL I SEE, ZOLA...

...IS ANOTHER MADMAN...
...WHO HASN'T LEARNED...
...WHAT HAPPENS TO *TYRANTS!*

YOU ADMIRE HITLER, ZOLA?
GO MEET HIM.

YOU'LL NEVER UNDERSTAND WHAT DRIVES A PERSON TO PICK UP THE SHIELD. KNOWING YOU'LL BE HATED FOR IT. THAT YOU'LL GET KNOCKED DOWN AND NOT GET BACK UP.
THAT THE VERY PEOPLE YOU'RE SWORN TO PROTECT WILL SEE IT AND CALL YOU THEIR ENEMY. IT'S A SPECIAL KINDA FOOL PICKS THIS THING UP AFTER EVERYTHING IT'S BEEN THROUGH.
AFTER EVERYTHING ***HE'S*** BEEN THROUGH.
SAME KINDA FOOL WHO'D TRY BUSTING INTO A ROCKET AS IT'S GETTING READY TO LEAVE THE SECOND LAYER OF EARTH'S ATMOSPHERE AND KILL HIM.
THING'S BURNING QUICK. NEED A WAY IN.

NGGGHHHH!
AGH!
THOOM
JUST IN TIME. ANY LONGER ON THAT THING AND I WOULDA BEEN A FIVE-BIRD ROAST.
≠HUFF≠ ≠HUFF≠
I GUESS THAT'S WHAT I GET FOR SPEECHIFYING.

I'D BE VERY DISAPPOINTED IF YOU SUDDENLY BECAME TIRED, CAPTAIN AMERICA. SURELY, YOU HAVE MORE FLIGHT IN YOU.

SUCH DRIVE.
SUCH STRENGTH.
SUCH HUBRIS.
ALL THAT RUNNING, ALL THAT FLIGHT. YOUR PEOPLE MUST BE TIRED, CAPTAIN AMERICA.
YOU CANNOT OUTLAST ARNIM ZOLA.
MY CONSCIOUSNESS IS ETERNAL. MY HUNGER IS BEYOND HUMAN COMPREHENSION. AND MY GENIUS WILL TRANSFORM YOUR WORLD.
RUNNING FROM WHIPS, RUNNING FROM CHAINS, RUNNING FROM AGENTS OF THE STATE, RUNNING FROM EACH OTHER.
RUNNING FROM AMERICA.
YOU ARE NOTHING IN THE SCHEME OF THE WORLD. YOU WILL WITHER AND DIE, JUST AS YOUR BELOVED IDEAL OF A COUNTRY SHALL FADE INTO THE DUST STORM OF HISTORY.
YOU'RE SERVING A COUNTRY THAT HAS SO RARELY SERVED YOU. DON'T YOU SEE THE FOLLY? SAVING AMERICA FROM ITSELF?

YOU ARE JUST ONE MAN.
WHAT CAN ONE MAN DO... BUT DIE?
THAT'S JUST IT, ZOLA.
I'M **NOT** ONE MAN.

I'M CAPTAIN AMERICA!

THE ALLEY-OOP...
...AND THE DUNK.
THE BOOSTERS SEEM TO HAVE CUT, BUT IT'S STILL HEAVY IN HERE. ONLY REASON I'M STANDING IS THE FLIGHT HOURS I'VE LOGGED.
DURING HIS SPEECH, ZOLA MENTION ANYTHING ABOUT TURNING THIS THING AROUND?
NO, HE DIDN'T GET TO THAT PART.
THERE HAS TO BE A WAY TO DISABLE THE CONTROLS, ALTER ITS FLIGHT PATTERN, STEER IT TO SAFETY...
NO TIME.
BUT I MADE A HOLE IN THE CEILING.
GOOD. BEEN ON MY FEET ALL DAY.

AWKWARD QUESTION.
SHOOT.
YOU GONNA BE "ASTONISHING CAPTAIN AMERICA" OR IS THAT GONNA BE ME?
REALLY, SAM? NOW?

IF YOU WANT MY OPINION, I THINK "UNCANNY CAPTAIN AMERICA" SUITS YOU.
NOT "SPECTACULAR CAPTAIN AMERICA"?
I MEAN, SURE. BUT I THINK YOU COULD REALLY PULL OFF "UNCANNY."
WHY DON'T YOU TAKE "UNCANNY"?

I'M JUST SAYING THAT--
SAM, LOOK OUT!
EUUUGH!
GOTCHA, BUDDY.

HOLD TIGHT! ROUGH LANDING COMING UP.
WHEN YOU'RE RIDING THE SHIELD LIKE A WAKEBOARD, THAT'S THE ONLY KIND!
SPLASH
HOW 'BOUT THIS? NO ADJECTIVES. WE'RE BOTH JUST...CAPTAIN AMERICA.
I COULD GET BEHIND THAT.
YEAH, THAT COULD WORK.

HARLEM.
LATER.
A SHAME, SAM WILSON.
YOU WOULD'VE MADE A GREAT WAKANDAN. PERHAPS A BETTER LEADER THAN MY BROTHER.
APOLLO
INSTEAD, THEY WILL TEAR YOU TO PIECES.
BUT WHO KNOWS? MAYBE YOU WIN. AND MAYBE WAKANDA FALLS FOREVER.
AND SO THE STARTING GUN HAS FIRED.

A SACRIFICE TO BLESS THE NEW CONTEST.
WELCOME, MY CLOSEST FRIENDS AND DEAREST ENEMIES, TO THE CENTURY GAME.
THE RULES ARE SIMPLE. WE KNOW THEM. WE LIVE THEM. ARE YOU PREPARED TO BEGIN?
YES.
YOUR STARPOINTS AWAIT. SOME OLD, SOME NEW. YOUR MOVES, AS EVER, ARE AT YOUR DISCRETION. THE WORLD IS OURS.
TO BUILD.
TO BREAK.
TO BURN.
LET A NEW DAY DAWN.

CULLY HAMNER & DAVID CURIEL
CAPTAIN AMERICA #0 SPIDER-MAN VARIANT

ADAM HUGHES
CAPTAIN AMERICA #0 VARIANT

JIM CHEUNG & JAY DAVID RAMOS
CAPTAIN AMERICA #0 VARIANT

ALEX ROSS
CAPTAIN AMERICA #0 SAM WILSON COVER

CAPTAIN AMERICA: SENTINEL OF LIBERTY #1

THE FORGE.
1941.
THIS IS WHAT I KNOW.

I KNOW WAR. HOW IT CAN TWIST THE HONORABLE INTO CRIMINALS AND THE COWARDLY INTO HEROES.
I KNOW FRIENDSHIP. HOW HOPE IN ONE ANOTHER BONDS FREE PEOPLE WHEN WE'RE DROWNING IN BLOOD.
I KNOW HATE. HOW IT BESTOWS POWER TO THE DESPERATE AND MAKES THE MOST BRILLIANT MIND ROT FROM THE INSIDE.
I KNOW THE MISSION. THE ONE THAT NEVER ENDS.
"STAND FOR THOSE WHO CAN'T."

I KNOW *DEVASTATION.* HOW OFTEN PEOPLE VISIT IT ON ONE ANOTHER-- AND THEMSELVES-- IN THE SERVICE OF POWER.
I KNOW *LOVE.* HOW IT CALMS THE HEART EVEN WHEN IT'S ABSENT.
AND MORE THAN ANYTHING...
...I KNOW *THE DREAM.*
AS FOR WHAT I *DON'T* KNOW?

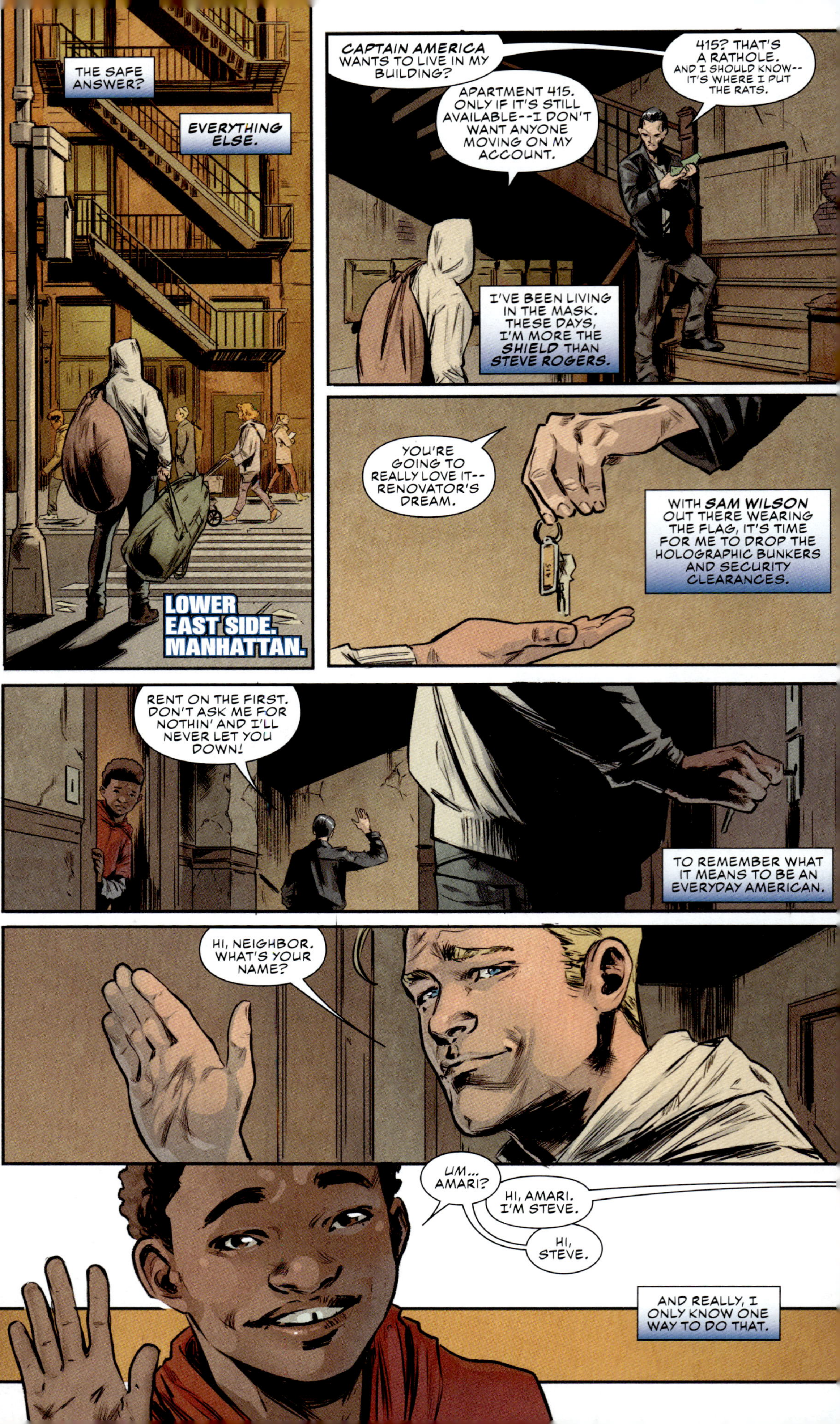
THE SAFE ANSWER?
EVERYTHING ELSE.
LOWER EAST SIDE. MANHATTAN.
CAPTAIN AMERICA WANTS TO LIVE IN MY BUILDING?
APARTMENT 415. ONLY IF IT'S STILL AVAILABLE--I DON'T WANT ANYONE MOVING ON MY ACCOUNT.
415? THAT'S A RATHOLE. AND I SHOULD KNOW--IT'S WHERE I PUT THE RATS.
I'VE BEEN LIVING IN THE MASK. THESE DAYS, I'M MORE THE SHIELD THAN STEVE ROGERS.
YOU'RE GOING TO REALLY LOVE IT--RENOVATOR'S DREAM.
WITH SAM WILSON OUT THERE WEARING THE FLAG, IT'S TIME FOR ME TO DROP THE HOLOGRAPHIC BUNKERS AND SECURITY CLEARANCES.
415
RENT ON THE FIRST. DON'T ASK ME FOR NOTHIN' AND I'LL NEVER LET YOU DOWN!
TO REMEMBER WHAT IT MEANS TO BE AN EVERYDAY AMERICAN.
HI, NEIGHBOR. WHAT'S YOUR NAME?
UM... AMARI?
HI, AMARI. I'M STEVE.
HI, STEVE.
AND REALLY, I ONLY KNOW ONE WAY TO DO THAT.

I NEED TO COME HOME.
JUST A NOTHING TENEMENT. FORGOTTEN. UNREMEMBERED. IF THE SMITHSONIAN KNEW THIS WAS WHERE I GREW UP, THEY'D TURN IT INTO A MUSEUM.
THE CAPTAIN AMERICA HOUSE.
FORTUNATELY, THERE'S ENOUGH OF MY PAST THAT REMAINS CLASSIFIED TO AFFORD ME THIS ONE BIT OF PRIVACY.
KITCHEN
BOOKS
NOTHING ABOUT IT IS THE SAME.
POP!
EVERYTHING ABOUT IT IS THE SAME.
SO WHAT DO I KNOW? THAT IN ALL OF THIS BEAUTIFUL LAND, SEA TO SHINING SEA...
...THIS IS WHERE I BELONG.

MY MORNINGS ALL START THE SAME WAY.
A JOG AROUND THE ISLAND.
AND SHARON WOULD SAY I CAN ONLY THINK WHEN I'M PUNCHING NAZIS OR MOVING FASTER THAN SEVENTY MILES PER HOUR ON FOOT.
BUCKY THINKS I'M ONLY DOING THIS BECAUSE SHARON'S BEEN CALLED AWAY ON SECRET BUSINESS.
BUT THERE'S A PEACE IN SOLITUDE.
AND JOY IN COMMUNITY.
THIRTY-TWO MILES.
WITH THE SHIELD ALWAYS POINTED TOWARD THEM.

THIRTY-TWO MILES.
I BRING THE SHIELD WITH ME. FOLKS ARE ALWAYS MORE EXCITED ABOUT THE SHIELD.
WHICH, AFTER THE LAST FEW YEARS OF GRAND DIRECTORS AND HATE-MONGERS AND THE RED SKULL, SUITS ME JUST FINE.
THEY SHOULDN'T SEE *ME* WHEN THEY SEE THE STARS AND STRIPES.
THEY SHOULD SEE *THEMSELVES.*
TO REMIND THEM--AND MYSELF--OF THE GREATEST LESSON I'VE LEARNED SINCE I WOKE UP FROM THE ICE.
THIS SHIELD BELONGS TO *ALL OF US.*
OF COURSE, SOME LESSONS AREN'T SO EASILY LEARNED...

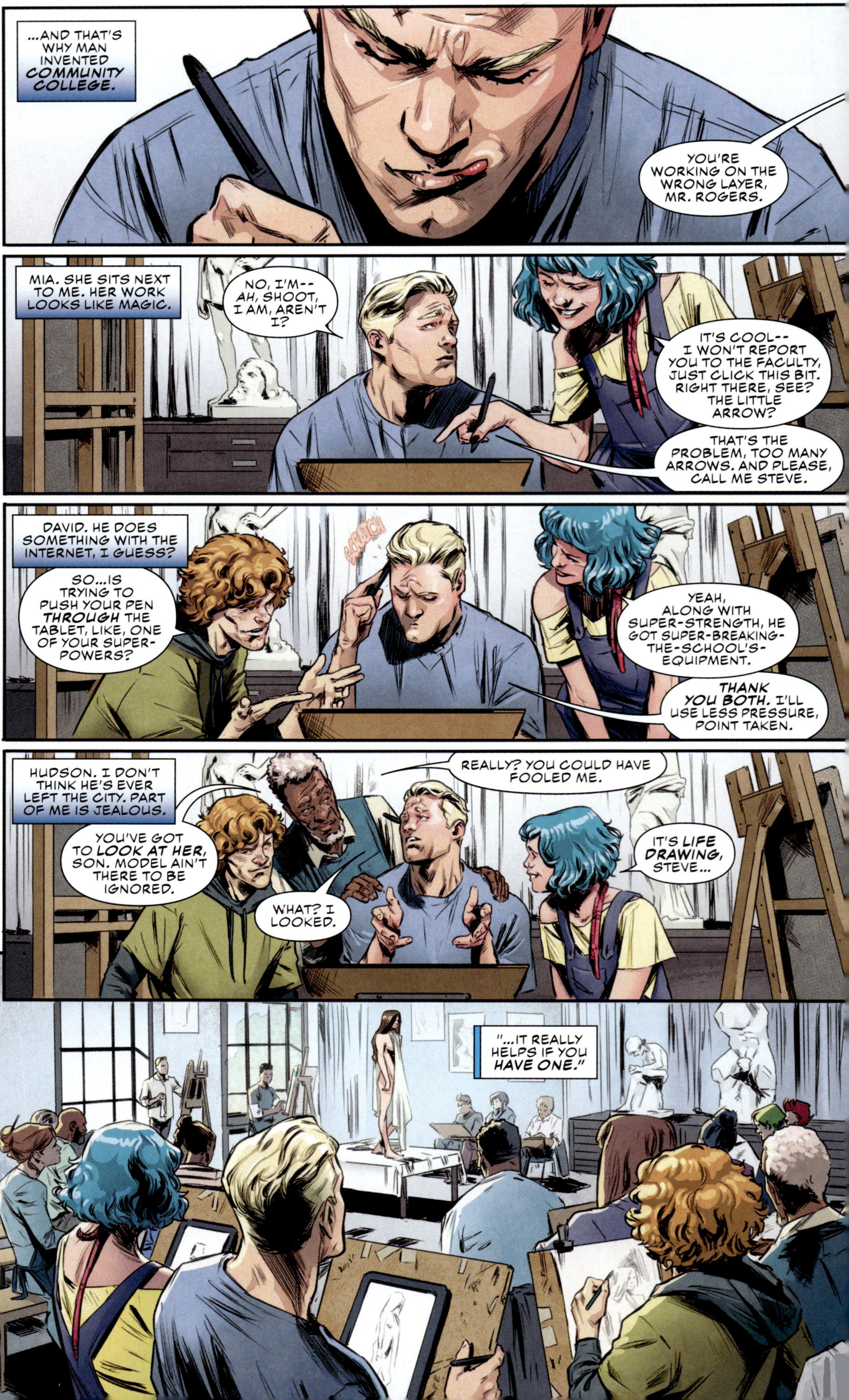
...AND THAT'S WHY MAN INVENTED COMMUNITY COLLEGE.
YOU'RE WORKING ON THE WRONG LAYER, MR. ROGERS.
MIA. SHE SITS NEXT TO ME. HER WORK LOOKS LIKE MAGIC.
NO, I'M-- AH, SHOOT, I AM, AREN'T I?
IT'S COOL-- I WON'T REPORT YOU TO THE FACULTY, JUST CLICK THIS BIT. RIGHT THERE, SEE? THE LITTLE ARROW?
THAT'S THE PROBLEM, TOO MANY ARROWS. AND PLEASE, CALL ME STEVE.
DAVID. HE DOES SOMETHING WITH THE INTERNET, I GUESS?
SCRATCH
SO...IS TRYING TO PUSH YOUR PEN THROUGH THE TABLET, LIKE, ONE OF YOUR SUPER-POWERS?
YEAH, ALONG WITH SUPER-STRENGTH, HE GOT SUPER-BREAKING-THE-SCHOOL'S-EQUIPMENT.
THANK YOU BOTH. I'LL USE LESS PRESSURE, POINT TAKEN.
HUDSON. I DON'T THINK HE'S EVER LEFT THE CITY. PART OF ME IS JEALOUS.
REALLY? YOU COULD HAVE FOOLED ME.
YOU'VE GOT TO LOOK AT HER, SON. MODEL AIN'T THERE TO BE IGNORED.
WHAT? I LOOKED.
IT'S LIFE DRAWING, STEVE...
"...IT REALLY HELPS IF YOU HAVE ONE."

I'D ALMOST FORGOTTEN WHAT IT WAS LIKE TO HAVE FRIENDS. CIVILIAN, NON-SUPER-SUITED, EARTHBORN, REGULAR, ACTUAL FRIENDS.
OKAY, BUT WHY THE METS?
UNDERDOGS.
YOU'RE IMPOSSIBLE.
I GET THAT A LOT.
BUT THEY'RE YOUNG.
THEY THINK THEY'RE WISE--AND THEY ARE, IN THEIR OWN WAY--BUT THE OLD MAN IN ME KNOWS A GULF SEPARATES US THAT I CAN NEVER QUITE CROSS.
YOU SHOULD HAVE SEEN HER IN PERSON! FRANKLIN MIGHT HAVE BEEN PRESIDENT, BUT SHE COMMANDED THE ROOM.
ELEANOR ROOSEVELT?
SHE WAS A DISH!
I KNOW BETTER THAN ANYONE THAT THE PAST DOESN'T STAY IN THE PAST.
THAT IT REPEATS.
YOU KNOW, I USED TO GET BULLIED IN THIS SAME ALLEY.
LET ME TEACH YOU WHAT I'VE LEARNED SINCE.
THAT YOU CAN ONLY SEE IT PROPERLY WITH TIME.
RADIO TWO, CHECKING IN.
ANYONE INTERESTED IN TEA AND A SUNRISE? OVER.
THEY CALL US THE GREATEST GENERATION...

...BUT WE CALL OURSELVES RADIO COMPANY.
RADIO FOUR, STILL UP. SO'S THE MOON, SO YOU'LL HAVE TO REPORT BACK ON THAT SUNRISE. HOW HAVE YOU BEEN, ROGER? OVER.
ROGER AUBREY, THE MIGHTY DESTROYER. SEE HOW HE KVETCHES. OVER.
BONES HURT. BREATHING HURTS. EVERYTHING HURTS. SERUM'S BEEN WORKING THIS OLD BLOODSTREAM FOR EIGHTY YEARS. WE DIDN'T ALL GET A SPA DAY IN THE ARCTIC SEA. OVER.
AT LEAST I'M NOT IN A COUNTRY THAT'S ABOUT TO THROW THE WORLD'S MOST GARISH BIRTHDAY FOR ITSELF. OVER.
HAR. YOU ARE VERY SPECIFICALLY NOT INVITED, FOR OBVIOUS REASONS.
OVER.
IS THAT STEVE? SHOULDN'T YOU BE PREPARING FOR TOMORROW? IT'S YOUR BIRTHDAY TOO, ISN'T IT? WHY ARE YOU JAWING WITH US MERE MORTALS? OVER.
JOHN, REMIND ME AGAIN--HOW CAN YOU CALL YOURSELF A MORTAL WHEN YOU'VE BEEN SHOT FOURTEEN TIMES? OVER.
NURSES LIKE YOU, PAM. EVER SINCE KOREA, YOU ALWAYS KEPT MY BLOOD PUMPING. OVER.
7--9-- 43--8-- 23--71--
COMPANY, CUT THE CHATTER FOR A MOMENT. YOU HEAR THAT? OVER.
--15-- 1--11--15-- 75--81--
SOUNDS LIKE AN OLD NUMBERS STATION? CODE FOR SOMETHING WITH NO ONE TO HEAR IT. BEEN AROUND SINCE WE WERE FIGHTING FIT. OVER.
EXCEPT THAT THIS WASN'T BROADCASTING YESTERDAY.
IT'S NEW. OVER.
--17-- 10--7-- 63--24-- 12--
SO...WE'VE GOT A MYSTERY ON OUR HANDS, IS WHAT YOU'RE SAYING? DON'T TEASE ME, I'VE COMPLETED EVERY NEW YORK TIMES PUZZLE PAGE FOR THE LAST THIRTY YEARS. OVER.
6--12-- 14--98-- 74--8--
THIS IS ALMOST 100 PERCENT A WASTE OF TIME... BUT I ONLY SLEEP FOUR HOURS A NIGHT, SO WHY NOT? OVER.
WELL, CAP, WHAT DO YOU SAY? IS THIS WORTH THE TIME? OVER.
RADIO COMPANY.
ASSEMBLE.

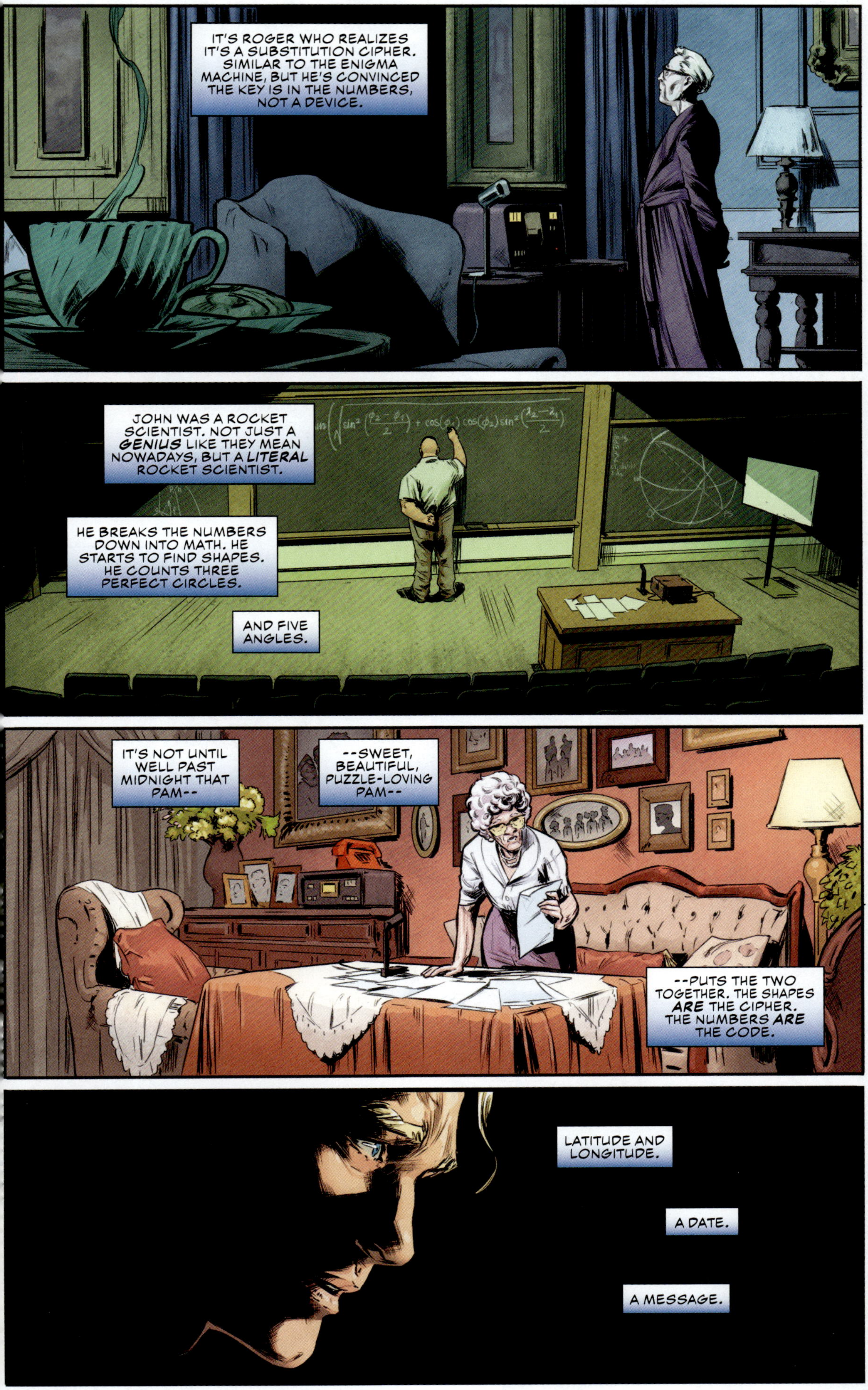
IT'S ROGER WHO REALIZES IT'S A SUBSTITUTION CIPHER. SIMILAR TO THE ENIGMA MACHINE, BUT HE'S CONVINCED THE KEY IS IN THE NUMBERS, NOT A DEVICE.
JOHN WAS A ROCKET SCIENTIST. NOT JUST A GENIUS LIKE THEY MEAN NOWADAYS, BUT A LITERAL ROCKET SCIENTIST.
HE BREAKS THE NUMBERS DOWN INTO MATH. HE STARTS TO FIND SHAPES. HE COUNTS THREE PERFECT CIRCLES.
AND FIVE ANGLES.
IT'S NOT UNTIL WELL PAST MIDNIGHT THAT PAM--
--SWEET, BEAUTIFUL, PUZZLE-LOVING PAM--
--PUTS THE TWO TOGETHER. THE SHAPES ARE THE CIPHER. THE NUMBERS ARE THE CODE.
LATITUDE AND LONGITUDE.
A DATE.
A MESSAGE.

Opening move
SOMETHING'S STARTING.
SOMETHING DEADLY.
Revolution
New York City
HAPPENING HERE.
The Fourth of July
Opening move
HAPPENING NOW.

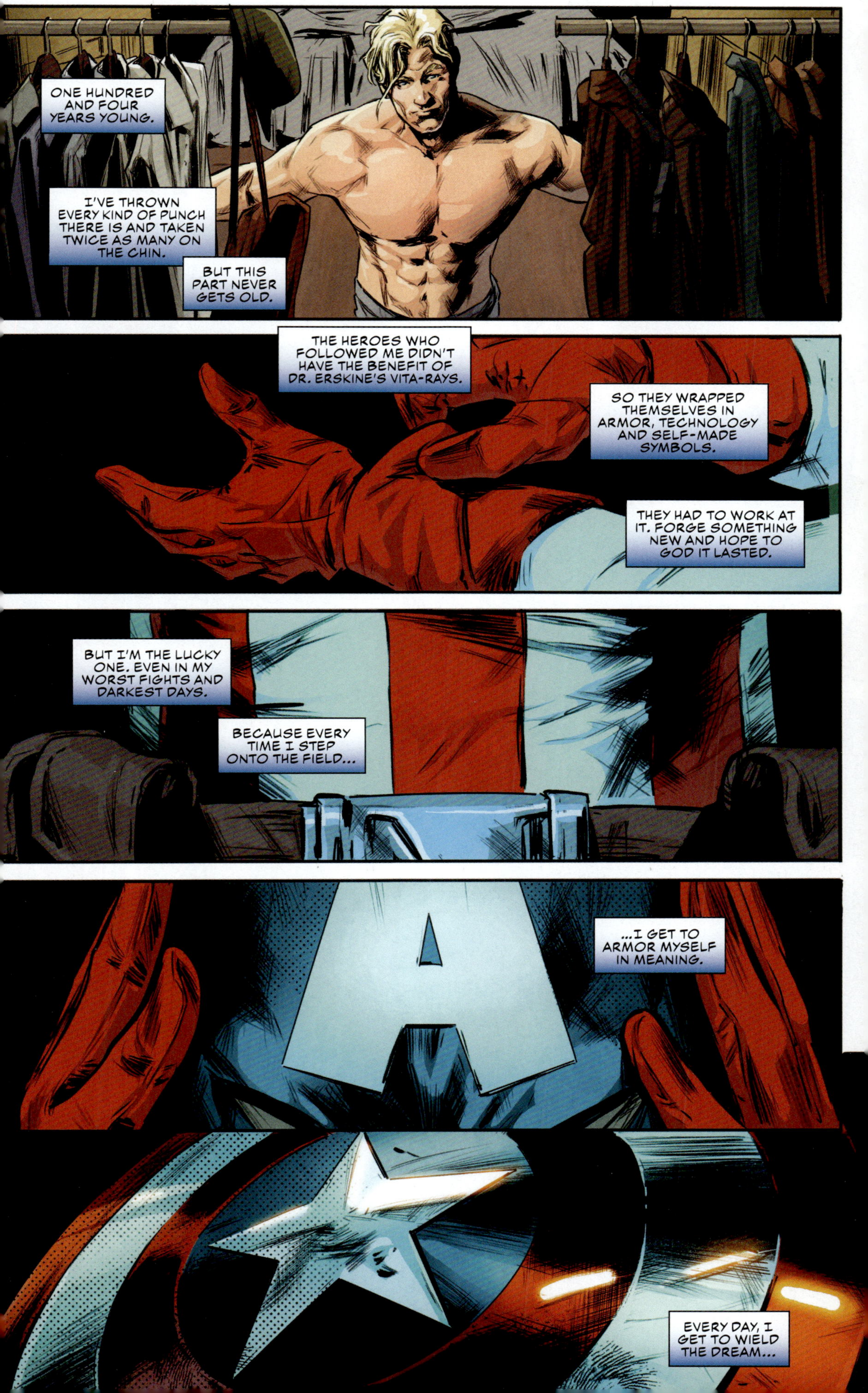
ONE HUNDRED AND FOUR YEARS YOUNG.
I'VE THROWN EVERY KIND OF PUNCH THERE IS AND TAKEN TWICE AS MANY ON THE CHIN.
BUT THIS PART NEVER GETS OLD.
THE HEROES WHO FOLLOWED ME DIDN'T HAVE THE BENEFIT OF DR. ERSKINE'S VITA-RAYS.
SO THEY WRAPPED THEMSELVES IN ARMOR, TECHNOLOGY AND SELF-MADE SYMBOLS.
THEY HAD TO WORK AT IT. FORGE SOMETHING NEW AND HOPE TO GOD IT LASTED.
BUT I'M THE LUCKY ONE. EVEN IN MY WORST FIGHTS AND DARKEST DAYS.
BECAUSE EVERY TIME I STEP ONTO THE FIELD...
...I GET TO ARMOR MYSELF IN MEANING.
EVERY DAY, I GET TO WIELD THE DREAM...

...AND MAKE IT REAL.
UNLIMITED

UNLIMITED
happy
4TH of July
4TH
UNITED STATES
Happy

SEVEN HOURS AND NOTHING BUT CELEBRATION. YOU SURE THIS SIGNAL'S LEGIT?
I'M NOT TAKING ANY CHANCES. EIGHT-AND-A-HALF MILLION PEOPLE, BUCK. AND THEY'RE ALL ON THE STREETS TODAY.
CHOOM
AND ONLY ABOUT 1.5 MILLION OF 'EM ARE DRESSED LIKE YOU. HAPPY BIRTHDAY, STEVE-- LOOKS LIKE THE WORLD'S GOT CAP FEVER AGAIN.
THEN WE BETTER NOT LET THEM DOWN.
COMMS CHECK. DON'T GET DISTRACTED BY THE PARADE.
LOUD AND CLEAR. DON'T GET HIT BY FIREWORKS.
COME ON, STEVE.
WHILE YOU WERE IN THE ICE, I WAS RUNNING COVERT ASSIGNMENTS AGAINST EVERY SUPER-POWERED TARGET ON EARTH.
NINJAS AVOID ME AT ALL COSTS. I FOUGHT WOLVERINE TO A STANDSTILL. LOKI ONCE TRIED TO TRICK ME AND ENDED UP WITH A BROKEN JAW.
I MAY NOT BE THE WINTER SOLDIER ANYMORE, BUT THAT'S THE ONE BENEFIT OF A LIFE OF VIOLENCE.
MY EYES ARE ***ALWAYS*** OPEN.
TARGET ON THE EAST RIVER. FIREWORKS BARGE. PICKING UP A STRANGE ENERGY SIGNATURE-- ***ANTIMATTER EXPLOSIVE.*** HAVEN'T SEEN TECH LIKE THAT SINCE I WAS THE MAN ON THE WALL.
AND HAVEN'T SEEN THAT ***UNIFORM*** SINCE...
SINCE THE WAR. I SEE HIM TOO.
ISN'T ROGER, LIKE, 90 YEARS OLD? AND BRIAN'S BEEN DEAD SINCE 1953.
YEAH. THIS IS SOMEONE NEW.
AND HE'S GONNA REGRET TAKING THE COLORS OF MEN I ***RESPECT.***

IN 1941, BRIAN FALSWORTH INFILTRATED THE GERMAN LINE UNDER AN ASSUMED NAME. HE WAS THE SON OF HEROES, HOPING TO BE ONE HIMSELF.
WHEN HE WAS CAPTURED, THE NAZIS MADE THE MISTAKE OF JAILING HIM WITH DR. ERIC SCHMITT, A GERMAN PATRIOT AND OLD FRIEND OF DR. ERSKINE'S.
WITHIN A MONTH, WITH ONLY THE SCRAPS AVAILABLE TO THEM IN THE CAMPS, DR. SCHMITT HAD MADE BRIAN A SUPER-SOLDIER.
THE DESTROYER.
WE FOUGHT SIDE BY SIDE OVER IN ENGLAND. HE LATER TOOK HIS FATHER'S NAME, UNION JACK, WHILE HIS BOYFRIEND, ROGER AUBREY, TOOK UP BRIAN'S MANTLE.
BRIAN DIED IN 1953, AND LEFT BEHIND A LEGACY OF HEROISM. REGARDLESS OF WHO WORE IT, THAT MASK STRUCK FEAR IN THE HEART OF FASCISTS FOR A CENTURY.
THIS GUY THINKS HE CAN TURN THAT LEGACY INTO A SYMBOL FOR WHATEVER TERRORIST AGENDA HE'S PEDDLING.
HE THINKS HISTORY ISN'T WATCHING. AND HECK, MAYBE IT ISN'T.
BUT I AM.

KRACK!
DROP THE DETONATOR. THIS CAN END WITHOUT ANY MORE VIOLENCE.
BUT YOU HAVE TO TAKE OFF THAT SUIT.
IT DOESN'T BELONG TO YOU.
HEH. YOU ACTUALLY SHOWED, YOU NEOFASCIST TRASH PILE. AND HERE I THOUGHT THE BOSS WAS BLUFFING.
I LOVE THE UNEARNED CONFIDENCE. BUT THIS IS SO MUCH BIGGER THAN YOU.
CLICK
TONIGHT IS THE TRUE START OF THE TWENTY-FIRST CENTURY. THE REVOLUTION IS COMING, AND THE WHOLE CITY'S GONNA BURN.
YOU'RE CRASHING A CELEBRATION, CAPTAIN AMERICA.
SO LET'S MAKE IT A DAMN PARTY, HUH? TELL ME SOMETHING.
YOU LIKE FIREWORKS?

I HIT HIM WITH THE FULL FORCE OF THE SHIELD ND IT JUST MADE HIM COCKIER.
SO HE'S GOT MY STRENGTH, ROGER'S ATTITUDE AND THOR'S LIGHTNING. GREAT.
BUCK, I COULD USE SOME COVERING FIRE.
TRYING! BUT MY ULLETS CAN'T ET THROUGH THE ANTI-MATTER!
MIGHT BE ABLE TO MAKE THE KILL SHOT THOUGH.
BUCKY, NO!
AH, BUCKY. GANG'S ALL HERE.
ZZZZZAAM!
MY SHIELD IS FORGED FROM A VIBRANIUM-STEEL ALLOY. ONLY ONE IN THE WORLD. IT CAN ABSORB NEARLY INFINITE KINETIC ENERGY.
IT TAKES A DARN MIRACLE TO PUT A DENT IN IT. BUT ALL IT'S DOING RIGHT NOW IS KEEPING ME STANDING. AND JUST BARELY.
YOU GET IT YET, YOU DISGUSTING RELIC?
IT'S TOO LATE FOR THIS CITY. BUT IT'S NOT TOO LATE FOR YOU.
RUN AWAY, CAPTAIN AMERICA...

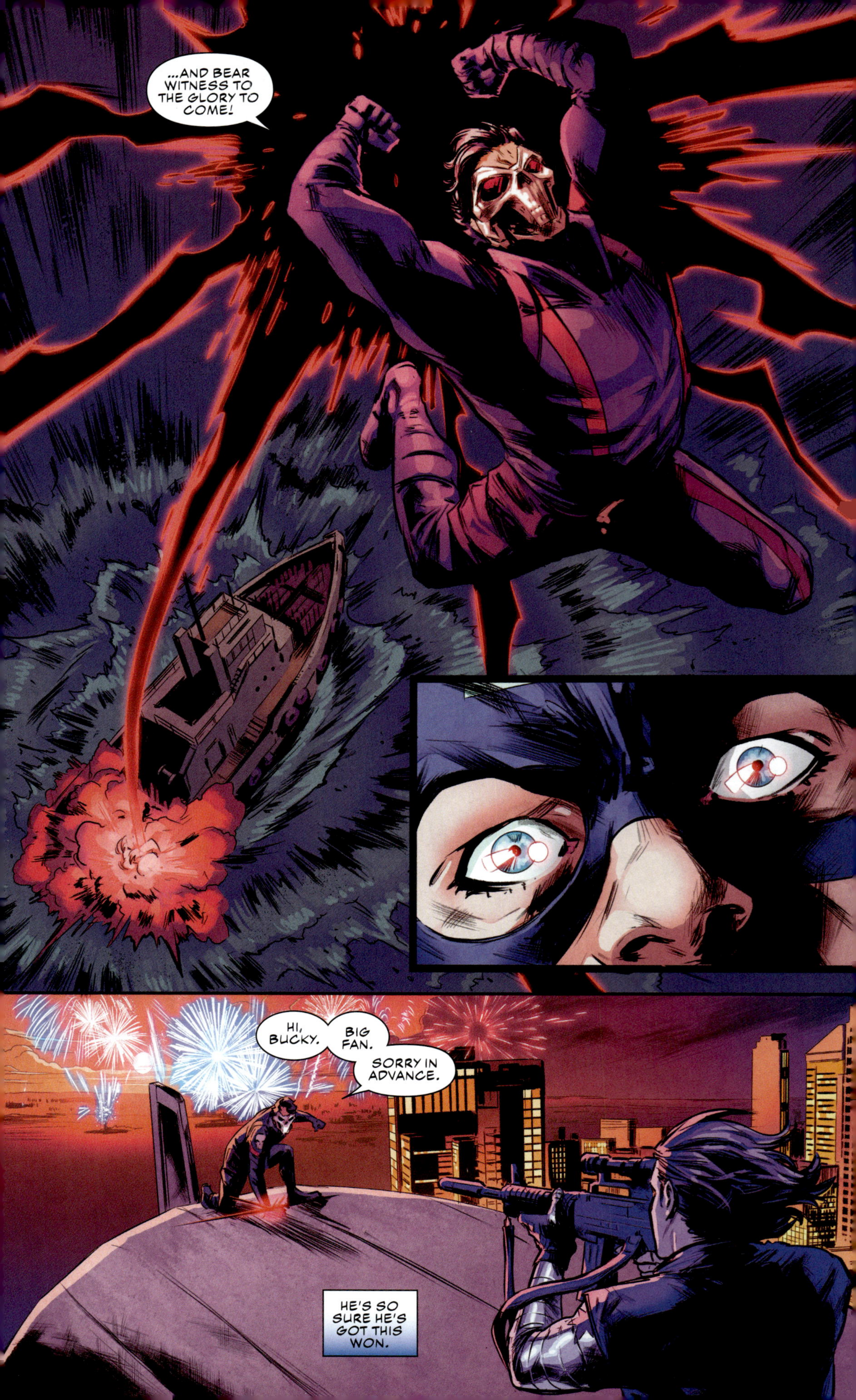
...AND BEAR WITNESS TO THE GLORY TO COME!
HI, BUCKY.
BIG FAN.
SORRY IN ADVANCE.
HE'S SO SURE HE'S GOT THIS WON.

AND THE FACTS BEAR HIM OUT.
HE'S A THOUSAND FEET UP, UNLEASHING ALL THIS POWER ON MY BEST FRIEND...
...AND I'M DOING LAPS IN THE EAST RIVER.
THAT'S THE THING ABOUT SUPER-SOLDIERS. IT'S WHY WE EXIST AT ALL. THE NAME ITSELF IS A CLUE. WE'RE NOT SOLDIERS. NOT REALLY.
WE'RE PSYOPS.
WE'RE AWE INCARNATE. WE'RE A DETERRENT.
YOU THERE! I NEED YOU TO RELEASE THAT BALLOON!
YOU HEARD CAP! LET HER FLY, BOYS!
WE WIN THE FIGHT BEFORE IT'S FOUGHT BY MAKING THE OTHER GUY RUN AWAY.
THIS NEW DESTROYER KNOWS THAT. HE'S USING HIS POWER EXPERTLY.
BUT HE'S YOUNG.
NEW ENOUGH TO THE GAME THAT HE HASN'T LEARNED THE FIRST THING ABOUT FIGHTING ME.
4th of July

I'LL RUN.
BUT NOT AWAY.
NEVER AWAY.

EVERY DAY SINCE THEY MADE ME, THEY TOLD ME STORIES ABOUT YOU.
THE GREAT CENTURY WEAPON.
THEY'LL TELL STORIES ABOUT ME AFTER TODAY.
AAAAAAAAAAHHHH!
AND YOU'LL BE NOTHING BUT--
KRAK
BIG TALK.
BUT YOU'RE WRONG, DIRTBAG.
IT'S YOU WHO'S GONNA BE NOTHING.
BRAKAKAKAKA

NO, BUCK.
THERE'S BEEN ENOUGH DESTRUCTION TODAY.
IT'S TIME FOR ANSWERS.

THE DEVICE HUMS LIKE SOMETHING FROM DIMENSION Z.
THAT SPECIAL KIND OF SONG THAT ONLY ELDRITCH WEAPONS CAN SING.
IT SOUNDS LIKE HATE.
I KNOW WHAT TO DO WITH HATE.
THE HECK IS THIS?
GOD HELP ME, IT'S ANOTHER GLOWING CRYSTAL. I'M GETTING REAL TIRED OF INFINITY STONES AND COSMIC CUBES, STEVE.
YOU AND ME BOTH.
SO OBSESSED WITH THE PAST...
...YOU CAN'T EVEN SEE THE FUTURE...WHEN YOU'RE HOLDING IT IN YOUR HANDS.
WHAT DOES THAT MEAN? SPEAK CLEARLY AND WE'LL MAKE SURE YOU'RE TAKEN SAFELY INTO CUSTODY.
WHO DO YOU WORK FOR? WHO SENT THE NUMBERS SIGNALS?
GOD... YOU'RE JUST SO... **PURE...**
...BUT I'M NOT WALKING AWAY FROM THIS.
NO ONE CAN.
EVER.

I FAILED TO EXECUTE HIS MOVE.
WHICH MEANS I'M LOOKING AT YOU WITH...DEAD EYES.
TALKING TO YOU... WITH DEAD LIPS...
WE CAN HELP YOU-- YOU JUST NEED TO--
SHUT UP. JUST... SHUT UP AND LISTEN.
THE SHIELD ISN'T WHAT YOU THINK.
IT'S NOT YOUR SYMBOL.
IT'S THEIRS.

WHAT DO I KNOW?
I KNOW MY ENEMY WILL TELL ME ANYTHING TO GET INSIDE MY HEAD.
I KNOW THE EASIEST WAY TO DESTROY THE DREAM IS WITH LIES.
AND I KNOW THE TRUTH WHEN I HEAR IT.

WHOEVER SENT THE DESTROYER JUST PUT THAT BOY'S BLOOD ON MY HANDS.
WITH HIS DYING BREATH, HE LEFT ME WITH A WAY TO MAKE THINGS RIGHT.
BUT ONLY IF I'M WILLING TO TAKE A HARD LOOK AT WHERE I CAME FROM.
WHAT I'VE BEEN WIELDING ALL THESE YEARS.
AND FACE WHATEVER I FIND THERE.
I KNOW AFTER A LIFETIME FIGHTING FOR THE DREAM...
...I HAVE TO WAKE UP.
IT'S LIKE VENTOLIN ALWAYS SAID, ALPINE.
THE LOST GLOVE IS HAPPY.
BUT I'M NOT LOST ANYMORE.

ONE DOWN.
1989
1951
BERLIN
FOUR TO GO.

MY FRIENDS. I APPRECIATE YOUR PATIENCE.
YOU'VE WAITED QUITE SOME TIME TO HEAR THIS RECORDING. BY THE TIME YOU ARE LISTENING TO THESE WORDS, I'LL HAVE... WELL...
...I'LL HAVE WON.
SO CONSIDER THIS A BIT OF BRAGGADOCIO. LIKE DEAR FIDEL WAS SO FOND OF. I KNOW IT'S A DARING GAMBIT. BUT I DO HOPE YOU'RE NOT TOO SURPRISED.
WE BOTH KNOW WHAT KIND OF GAME YOU'RE PLAYING.
WE BOTH KNOW WHAT I AM.
THE CLASSIC GAME, AS WE ALL KNOW, IS RIFE WITH PAWN SACRIFICE. AND THAT WILL BE WHAT YOU THINK I HAVE DONE.
BECAUSE YOU DESIGNED THIS WHOLE THING ON THE CLASSIC GAME, OF COURSE, THE ONLY GAME THAT MATTERED, BECAUSE IN ALL YOUR YEARS OF BOUNDLESS LIFE...
... YOU NEVER LEARNED TO PLAY CHECKERS.
SO I GOT ACROSS THE BOARD WHEN YOU WEREN'T LOOKING AND TURNED MY PAWN INTO A KING.
YOUR GREATEST FAILURE. YOUR ABSOLUTE DOWNFALL. I'VE PUT CAPTAIN AMERICA ON THE BOARD.
AND THAT'S JUST MY OPENER.
THE TWENTIETH CENTURY WAS A DRAW.
THE TWENTY-FIRST WILL BE PLAYED FOR KEEPS.
FORWARD THE REVOLUTION.

MARK BROOKS

CAPTAIN AMERICA #0 WRAPAROUND VARIANT

JOSHUA CASSARA & DIJJO LIMA

CAPTAIN AMERICA: SENTINEL OF LIBERTY #1 STORMBREAKERS VARIANT

TAURIN CLARKE

CAPTAIN AMERICA: SENTINEL OF LIBERTY #1 VARIANT

CAPTAIN AMERICA: SENTINEL OF LIBERTY #2

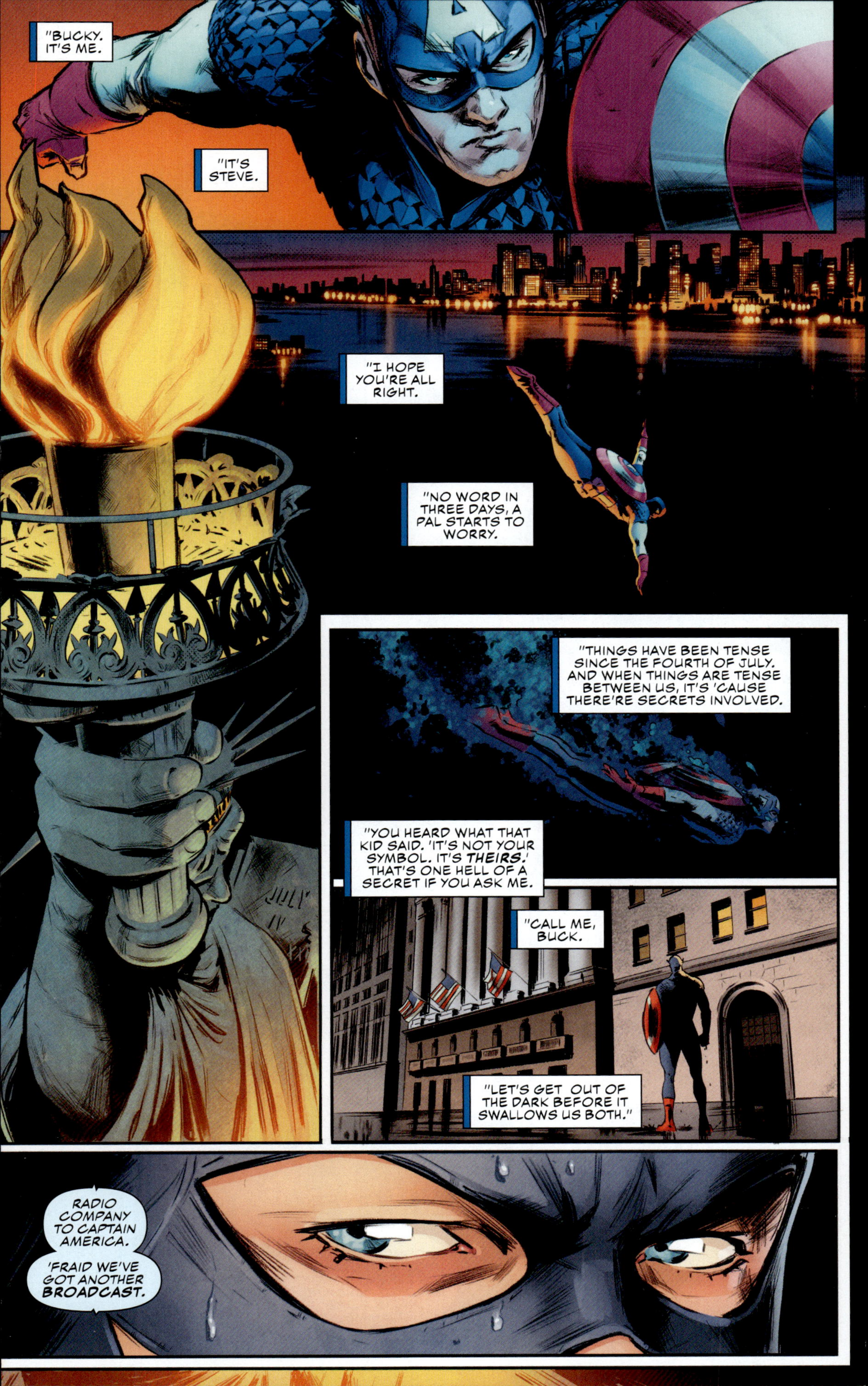
"BUCKY. IT'S ME.
"IT'S STEVE.
"I HOPE YOU'RE ALL RIGHT.
"NO WORD IN THREE DAYS, A PAL STARTS TO WORRY.
"THINGS HAVE BEEN TENSE SINCE THE FOURTH OF JULY. AND WHEN THINGS ARE TENSE BETWEEN US, IT'S 'CAUSE THERE'RE SECRETS INVOLVED.
"YOU HEARD WHAT THAT KID SAID. 'IT'S NOT YOUR SYMBOL. IT'S *THEIRS.*' THAT'S ONE HELL OF A SECRET IF YOU ASK ME.
"CALL ME, BUCK.
"LET'S GET OUT OF THE DARK BEFORE IT SWALLOWS US BOTH."
RADIO COMPANY TO CAPTAIN AMERICA.
'FRAID WE'VE GOT ANOTHER **BROADCAST.**

HOW MANY IS THAT THIS WEEK, ROGER?
THIS ONE MAKES FOUR. IT'S STILL RUNNING THROUGH THE DECODER WE'VE BUILT. THE GOOD NEWS IS, THERE HAVEN'T BEEN MORE SUPER HERO CHILDREN STEALING MY OLD MANTLE AS THE DESTROYER.
THE BAD NEWS IS, I'M BEGINNING TO SETTLE MY MIND ON SOMETHING OF A UNIFIED THEORY BETWEEN THESE NUMBER STATION DIRECTIVES.
POWER
NATO withdrawal from Symkaria Border Region.
MOVE 002
I'VE NOT SEEN A WAR MACHINE LIKE IT SINCE HYDRA, NOR A POLITICAL POWER CAPABLE OF THESE KINDS OF...MOVES. NOT EVER.
AUBREY'S RIGHT, STEVE. I'VE BEEN LOOKING AT THAT FIRST LINE, AND I THINK IT'S SOME KIND OF IDENTIFIER. MAYBE THE BOARD. MAYBE THE PLAYER.
WHOEVER THESE PEOPLE ARE, THEY'RE PLAYING ON THE BATTLEFIELDS OF POWER, OF WEALTH, OF INDUSTRY AND POPULAR ART AND EVEN REVOLUTION. WHICH SEEMS PRETTY ESOTERIC TO ME--
THAT'S JUST BECAUSE WE DON'T UNDERSTAND THE RULES YET, JOHN.
REVOLUTION
Jiangsu Province protest wave.
MOVE 009
WHAT CAN I SAY? I THINK BETTER WHEN I'M MOVING.
A BRUTAL THING TO SAY TO AN ALMOST-CENTENARIAN. IF ONLY PEOPLE KNEW WHAT A RIGHT BASTARD CAPTAIN AMERICA COULD BE.
GLASS HOUSES, ROGER. YOU'RE THE ONLY MAN I EVER MET WHO ENJOYED PUNCHING NAZIS MORE THAN ME.

I'M RATHER CONVINCED IT'S ALL A GAME.
THESE ARE PEOPLE'S LIVES, ROGER. THE FATES OF ENTIRE COUNTRIES. WHAT KIND OF GAME IS THAT?
A GAME OF HISTORY ITSELF. SHAPING. REWORKING. COMPETING.
MONEY
ECB interest rates down.
Market crisis point
T-minus 2 months.
MOVE 003
LOVE
Restorationism is in.
Jean-Pierre at the Louvre.
MOVE 006
BUT YOU CAN'T PUNCH YOUR WAY OUT OF A PUZZLE.
GOD LOVE YOU, STEVE, BUT YOU'RE HIS EXCEPTION. US MERE MORTALS GOTTA KEEP WORKING IT OUT WITH OUR BRAINS.
I DON'T KNOW, PAM. I'VE SEEN SOME THINGS.
WELL, AFRAID THIS MOVE IS NO MORE SUPER-VILLAINOUS THAN THE LAST.
AND QUITE A BIT MORE CRYPTIC. WHAT IN BLOODY BLAZES IS THIS SUPPOSED TO MEAN?
MACHINE
Secure the Forge.
MOVE 011

THE FED
HAPPY HOUR 1600-2100
YOU NEED A HAND WITH THOSE DRINKS, MR. ROGERS? IT'S BEEN A CENTURY!
SORRY, MIA. I GUESS I'VE JUST BEEN IN MY HEAD A LITTLE THIS WEEK.
THE BURDEN OF THE ARTIST--THINK TOO MUCH, FORGIVE OURSELVES TOO LITTLE.
BUT THAT'S WHAT FRIENDS ARE FOR. SPILL THE TEA, CAP?
ER, CAN I CALL YOU CAP?
YOU CAN, DAVID. BUT STEVE'S BETTER.
NOT GIVING UP "MR. ROGERS" AND YOU CAN'T MAKE ME.
WHAT'S ON YOUR MIND, STEVE?
I...
THAT ATTACK LAST WEEK, HUDSON. THE GUY, THE BOMBER... HE WAS...SOMEONE'S KID. TWISTED OUT OF SHAPE BY PEOPLE WHO DIDN'T CARE WHETHER HE LIVED OR DIED.
AND BEFORE HE DIED, BEFORE THEY KILLED HIM, HE SAID SOMETHING THAT SHOOK ME UP.
"IT'S NOT YOUR SYMBOL. IT'S THEIRS."

HE WAS TALKING ABOUT THE SHIELD. THE SYMBOL I'VE SPENT MY WHOLE LIFE REPRESENTING. THE DREAM I'VE FOUGHT FOR EVERY DAY SINCE THE FORTIES.
HE KNEW SOMETHING I DIDN'T. AND IT MADE ME REALIZE HOW LITTLE I KNOW ABOUT THE THINGS... THE PEOPLE...WHO MADE ME.
HECK, I DON'T EVEN KNOW THE NAME OF THE PERSON WHO DESIGNED IT...
OH. I GOT YOU. I'M ALREADY ON IT.
SORRY?
TAP TAP TAP TAP
I TOLD YOU: I DO COMPUTERS. WHAT THAT ACTUALLY MEANS IS I HELP RUN THE LARGEST ARCHIVAL SEARCH DATABASE IN THE WORLD. AND MOST OF OUR CLIENTS ARE NATSEC, SO...
...AND... HERE...WE... GO.
DOCTOR DANIEL AGBOJE. MOST OF HIS FILE IS CLASSIFIED, BUT HE'S LISTED AS THE SHIELD'S DESIGNER ON THE OLD REQUISITION PAPERWORK.
IT SEEMS THAT SOMEONE NAMED MYRON MACLAIN DID THE ACTUAL INDUSTRIAL DESIGN--HE WAS A TANK MAKER? BUT THE ALLOY FINISHING WAS ALL THIS GUY NAMED AGBOJE. HE'S GOT EXACTLY ONE RECORDS PING AND ZERO CITIZENSHIP DATA.
KIND OF A DEAD TRAIL. SORRY, STEVE.
PLEASE DON'T BE. IT'S MORE THAN I HAD A MOMENT AGO. YOU REALLY DID THAT FROM YOUR CELL PHONE?
STARKTECH. NEXT TIME YOU SEE TONY, THANK HIM.
NO, I DON'T THINK I WILL.
CHEERS. TO FRIENDS. THE ONES WHO SHOW US THAT EVEN IN OUR DARKEST MOMENTS...

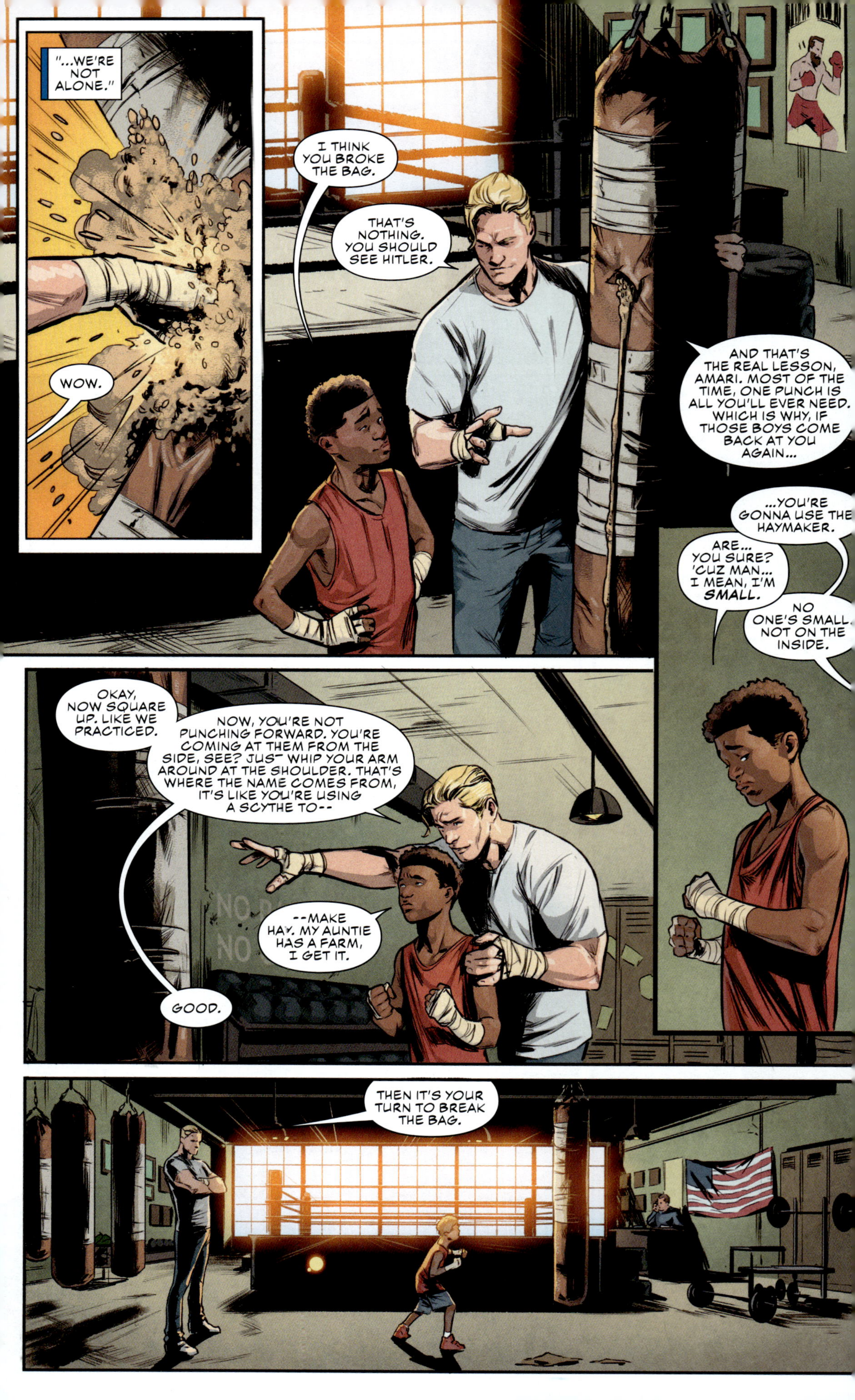
"...WE'RE NOT ALONE."
WOW.
I THINK YOU BROKE THE BAG.
THAT'S NOTHING. YOU SHOULD SEE HITLER.
AND THAT'S THE REAL LESSON, AMARI. MOST OF THE TIME, ONE PUNCH IS ALL YOU'LL EVER NEED. WHICH IS WHY, IF THOSE BOYS COME BACK AT YOU AGAIN...
...YOU'RE GONNA USE THE HAYMAKER.
ARE... YOU SURE? 'CUZ MAN... I MEAN, I'M **SMALL.**
NO ONE'S SMALL. NOT ON THE INSIDE.
OKAY, NOW SQUARE UP. LIKE WE PRACTICED.
NOW, YOU'RE NOT PUNCHING FORWARD. YOU'RE COMING AT THEM FROM THE SIDE, SEE? JUST WHIP YOUR ARM AROUND AT THE SHOULDER. THAT'S WHERE THE NAME COMES FROM, IT'S LIKE YOU'RE USING A SCYTHE TO--
--MAKE HAY. MY AUNTIE HAS A FARM, I GET IT.
GOOD.
THEN IT'S YOUR TURN TO BREAK THE BAG.

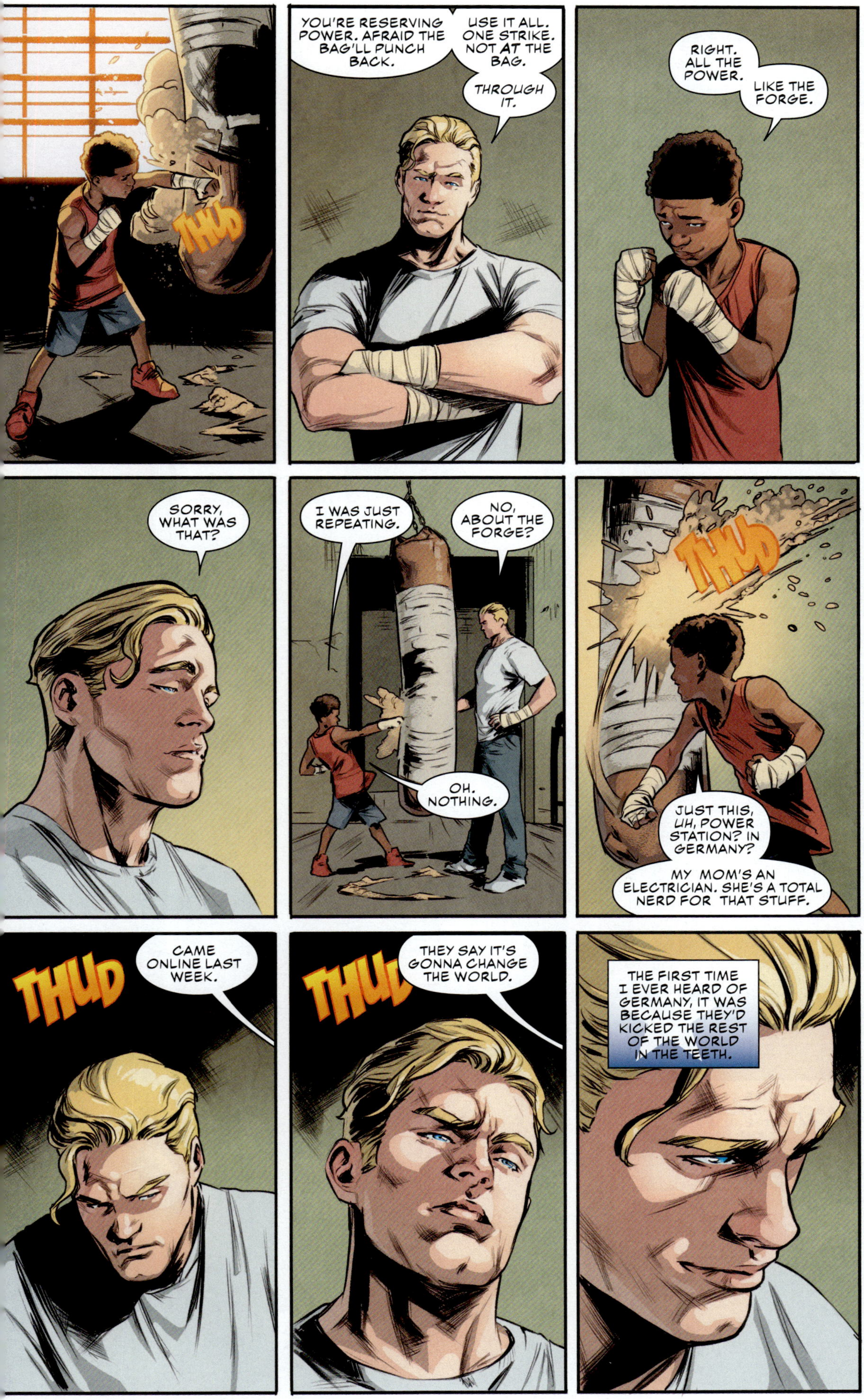
THUD
YOU'RE RESERVING POWER. AFRAID THE BAG'LL PUNCH BACK.
USE IT ALL. ONE STRIKE. NOT AT THE BAG.
THROUGH IT.
RIGHT. ALL THE POWER.
LIKE THE FORGE.
SORRY, WHAT WAS THAT?
I WAS JUST REPEATING.
NO, ABOUT THE FORGE?
OH. NOTHING.
THUD
JUST THIS, UH, POWER STATION? IN GERMANY?
MY MOM'S AN ELECTRICIAN. SHE'S A TOTAL NERD FOR THAT STUFF.
THUD
CAME ONLINE LAST WEEK.
THUD
THEY SAY IT'S GONNA CHANGE THE WORLD.
THE FIRST TIME I EVER HEARD OF GERMANY, IT WAS BECAUSE THEY'D KICKED THE REST OF THE WORLD IN THE TEETH.

IN THE DAYS SINCE, IT SEEMS THEY'RE MORE DETERMINED THAN EVER TO GIVE BACK. TO MAKE THINGS RIGHT. THAT RARE BULLY WHO ACTUALLY LEARNED THE LESSON.
AMARI'S MOM HAD IT RIGHT. ***THE FORGE***--A GREEN-ENERGY POWER PLANT BUILT ON EXPERIMENTAL TECHNOLOGY. IT LIGHTS UP HALF OF EUROPE. AN INCREDIBLE ACCOMPLISHMENT.
AND IF I'M RIGHT, THESE MADMEN HAVE MADE IT THEIR NEXT TARGET.
I CAN'T HELP BUT THINK OF BILL, WHO FLEW US OVER THE GARRISON ON WATZMANN, AND CHICK, WHO BLEW THE VAULT AT COLDITZ...
...AND ALL THE OTHER YOUNG MEN WHO TRUDGED ACROSS MILES OF SNOW TO BRING THE FIGHT TO BERLIN.
THOSE ALWAYS SEEMED LIKE SIMPLER TIMES.
BUT MAYBE THAT'S JUST BECAUSE I WAS SIMPLER BACK THEN.
THE MORE I LEARN ABOUT THE GOOD OLD DAYS, THE MORE I REALIZE: THE SECRETS DIDN'T BEGIN WHEN I CAME OUT OF THE ICE.
THEY WERE ON THE BATTLEFIELD WITH ME. I WAS CARRYING THEM.
I STILL DO.

BY THE TIME YOU GET THIS CLOSE TO A HOSTAGE SITUATION, YOU NORMALLY HEAR THE SPEECHES.
THE DEMANDS FOR MONEY AND POWER.
BUT THESE MADMEN DON'T NEED ANY OF THAT, DO THEY?
THEY HAVE WHAT THEY NEED.
UNLIMITED ENERGY AT THEIR FINGERTIPS.
AND THE ONLY WITNESSES AT THEIR MERCY, WHICH I'M BETTING FROM THE ALL-BLACK BATTLE ARMOR DOESN'T EXTEND VERY FAR.
WHICH MAKES THIS NEXT PART PRETTY STRAIGHT-FORWARD.

HE'S HERE!
ALL TITHED AGENTS...
...OPEN FIRE!
I BARELY CLOCK WHAT I SAY TO THE HOSTAGES. CALMING WORDS, BUT COMMANDING. DIRECTING THEM TO EVACUATE.
BUT MY MIND'S DISTRACTED. CATCHING THE DETAILS. TRYING TO LEARN WHO I'M FIGHTING HERE.
HYDRA SYMBOLOGY.
THE KUSARIGAMA TECHNIQUES OF A HAND NINJA.
THE KINETIC RESISTANT FABRIC OF AN A.I.M. ENCOUNTER SUIT.
ALL IN THE SAME UNIFORM.

THAT WORD HE SAID WHEN I ARRIVED. TITHED.
WHOEVER'S PLAYING THIS GAME, THEY'RE PULLING PAWNS FROM EVERY ORGANIZATION I'VE EVER FOUGHT. TRIBUTE UP THE CHAIN.
THIS IS YOUR ONLY WARNING, SIR.
STAND DOWN.
NO. NOT JUST THOSE I'VE FOUGHT.
THOSE I'VE FOUGHT ALONGSIDE.

ORTIZ! AGENT ORTIZ! I REMEMBER YOU! YOU'RE A GOOD MAN!
WHAT THE HELL ARE YOU DOING FIGHTING ALONGSIDE MADMEN LIKE A.I.M. AND THE HAND?
I'M FOLLOWING ORDERS.
WE ALL ARE.
IF THERE'S ONE THING I CAN'T STAND...

...IT'S MEN WHO JUST FOLLOW ORDERS.
THE FIGHT CLEARS MY HEAD. IT'S THE FIRST PEACE I'VE FELT IN A WEEK.
BUT THEN THE MYSTERY CREEPS BACK. THAT YOUNG KID'S DYING WORDS ECHOING FROM THE BACK OF MY MIND.
"IT'S NOT YOUR SYMBOL.

"IT'S THEIRS."

UNEXPECTED. BUT NOT UNWELCOME.
THE MACHINE MOTIONS TO... REDACT.
THE MONEY SECONDS THE MOTION.
THE POWER VOTES YES.
LOVE ABSTAINS.
WHO AM I TO STAND IN YOUR WAY?
THE REVOLUTION VOTES YES.

"REDACTION AUTHORIZED."
VOOSH
YOU WANT MY SYMBOL?

COME AND TAKE IT.

STAY DOWN, PAL. AND DON'T CALL SECURITY. AFTER ALL...
MADRIPOOR.
...I COULD'VE HIT YOU WITH THE METAL ONE.
HIGH ROLLERS
LADIES AND GENTLEMEN OF THE PRINCIPALITY TABLE, I APOLOGIZE FOR THE RUDE INTRUSION...
...BUT MY NAME IS BUCKY BARNES.
AND I'D LIKE TO BUY IN.

NAMES AREN'T REQUIRED, MR. BARNES. THIS IS A HIGH ROLLERS TABLE FOR WEALTHY AND DISCREET INDIVIDUALS, NOT A SOCIAL CLUB.
BUT YOUR MONEY IS WELCOME ALL THE SAME.
THE GAME IS BACCARAT.
GOOD, 'CUZ I'M REAL CRAP AT GO FISH.
BUT IF I'M BEING HONEST, I'M ONLY HERE BECAUSE I KNEW I COULD FIND YOU.
DON'T DO THIS, BARNES. NOT HERE.
SORRY, BUT WE DON'T HAVE TIME FOR SPYCRAFT. YOU AND I HAVE TO TALK STRAIGHT.
YOU WANT STRAIGHT TALK? I RUN THIS GAME FOR A REASON AND YOU'RE BLOWING MY COVER.
I'M MEETING YOU WHERE YOU LIVE. IN THE SHADOWS. BECAUSE THAT'S WHERE THE REAL WAR IS BEING FOUGHT.
A WAR AS OLD AS YOU AND ME.
FIVE SOLDIERS. FIVE POINTS OF A STAR. ALL FIGHTING FOR ONE MYSTERIOUS CAUSE.
AND YOU'RE ONE OF THEM.
SO TELL ME...

...WHO DO YOU REALLY WORK FOR, PEGGY CARTER?

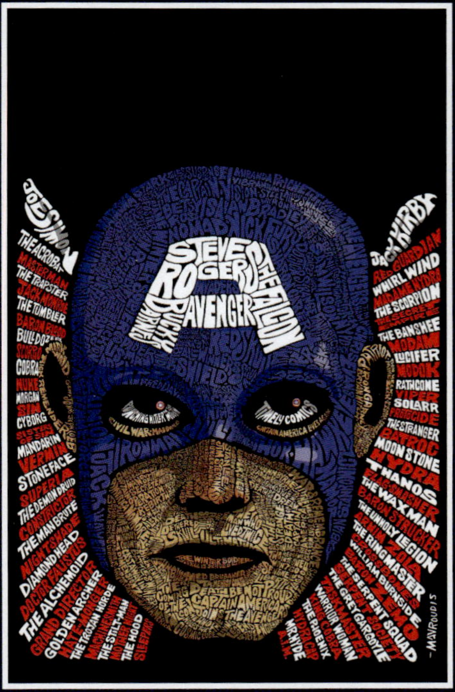

JOHN MAVROUDIS

CAPTAIN AMERICA: SENTINEL OF LIBERTY #1 VARIANT

LUCIANO VECCHIO

CAPTAIN AMERICA: SENTINEL OF LIBERTY #1 PRIDE VARIANT

JULIAN TOTINO TEDESCO

CAPTAIN AMERICA: SENTINEL OF LIBERTY #1 VARIANT

CAPTAIN AMERICA: SENTINEL OF LIBERTY #3

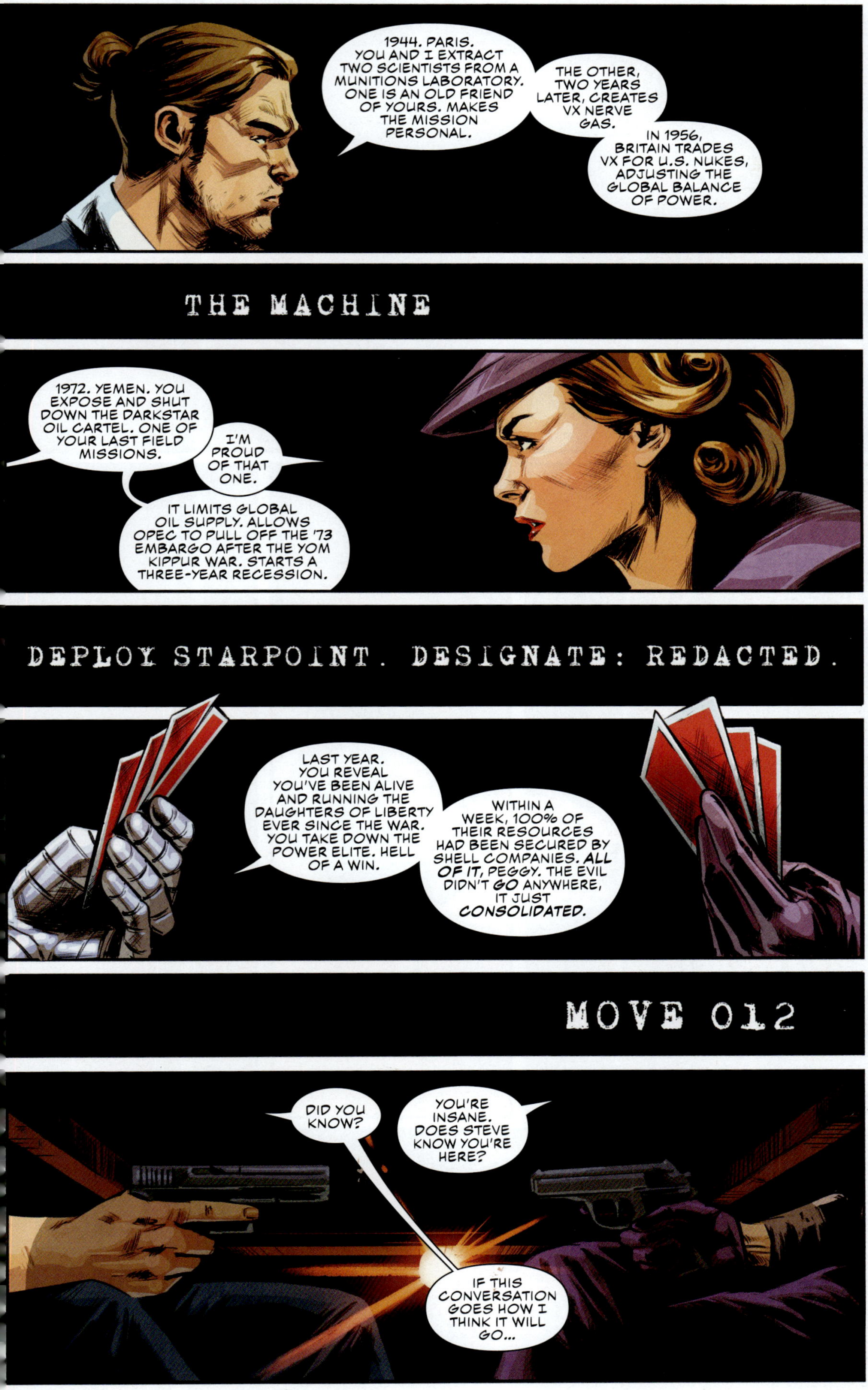
1944. PARIS. YOU AND I EXTRACT TWO SCIENTISTS FROM A MUNITIONS LABORATORY. ONE IS AN OLD FRIEND OF YOURS. MAKES THE MISSION PERSONAL.
THE OTHER, TWO YEARS LATER, CREATES VX NERVE GAS.
IN 1956, BRITAIN TRADES VX FOR U.S. NUKES, ADJUSTING THE GLOBAL BALANCE OF POWER.
THE MACHINE
1972. YEMEN. YOU EXPOSE AND SHUT DOWN THE DARKSTAR OIL CARTEL. ONE OF YOUR LAST FIELD MISSIONS.
I'M PROUD OF THAT ONE.
IT LIMITS GLOBAL OIL SUPPLY. ALLOWS OPEC TO PULL OFF THE '73 EMBARGO AFTER THE YOM KIPPUR WAR. STARTS A THREE-YEAR RECESSION.
DEPLOY STARPOINT. DESIGNATE: REDACTED.
LAST YEAR. YOU REVEAL YOU'VE BEEN ALIVE AND RUNNING THE DAUGHTERS OF LIBERTY EVER SINCE THE WAR. YOU TAKE DOWN THE POWER ELITE. HELL OF A WIN.
WITHIN A WEEK, 100% OF THEIR RESOURCES HAD BEEN SECURED BY SHELL COMPANIES. ALL OF IT, PEGGY. THE EVIL DIDN'T GO ANYWHERE, IT JUST CONSOLIDATED.
MOVE 012
DID YOU KNOW?
YOU'RE INSANE. DOES STEVE KNOW YOU'RE HERE?
IF THIS CONVERSATION GOES HOW I THINK IT WILL GO...

"...STEVE'S BETTER OFF STAYING THE HELL AWAY."
STEVEN ROGERS
THE FORGE. THE EUROPEAN UNION'S PREMIER GREEN ENERGY FACILITY.
BY ORDER OF THE OUTER CIRCLE
YOU HAVE BEEN REDACTED
HISTORY WILL NOT REMEMBER YOU

THE IMPACT SCRAPES ACROSS THE METAL LIKE NAILS ON THE WORLD'S BIGGEST CHALKBOARD.
I'VE ONLY HEARD THAT SOUND ONCE BEFORE.
THE FIRST TIME I FOUGHT LOGAN.
THIS MACHINE IS MADE OF VIBRANIUM, ADAMANTIUM OR SOMETHING JUST AS STRONG.
A DESCENDANT OF MY SHIELD, MAYBE.
EXHAUSTION CREEPS FROM MY ACHING ARM TO MY RESTLESS MIND.
I HEAR THE BOYS IN THE TWELFTH, STANDING TALL ALONG THE WESTERN FRONT.
NO GUARANTEE OF VICTORY. AN ENTIRE NATION OF FASCISTS STARING US DOWN, THROWING THEIR YOUNG AT US WHILE THEY HID IN THEIR CASTLES.
IT SNOWED ALONG THE RHINE FOR THREE WEEKS STRAIGHT.
WE SURVIVED THE WINTER.
I CAN SURVIVE THIS.

I THINK OF PFC BOWMAN, WHO WENT HAND TO HAND WITH A GERMAN BAYONET AND WON.
CPL YORKE, WHO CHALLENGED ME TO A LONG JUMP EVERY NIGHT.
BUCKY, RUNNING ACROSS ROOFTOPS, ALWAYS LOOKING FOR THE ONE UNSEEN ADVANTAGE.
NAMOR, WHO NEVER MET A THING MADE BY HUMAN HANDS THAT HE COULDN'T BEND TO FIGHT BACK AGAINST THEM.
JIM, WHO BURNED SO BRIGHT.

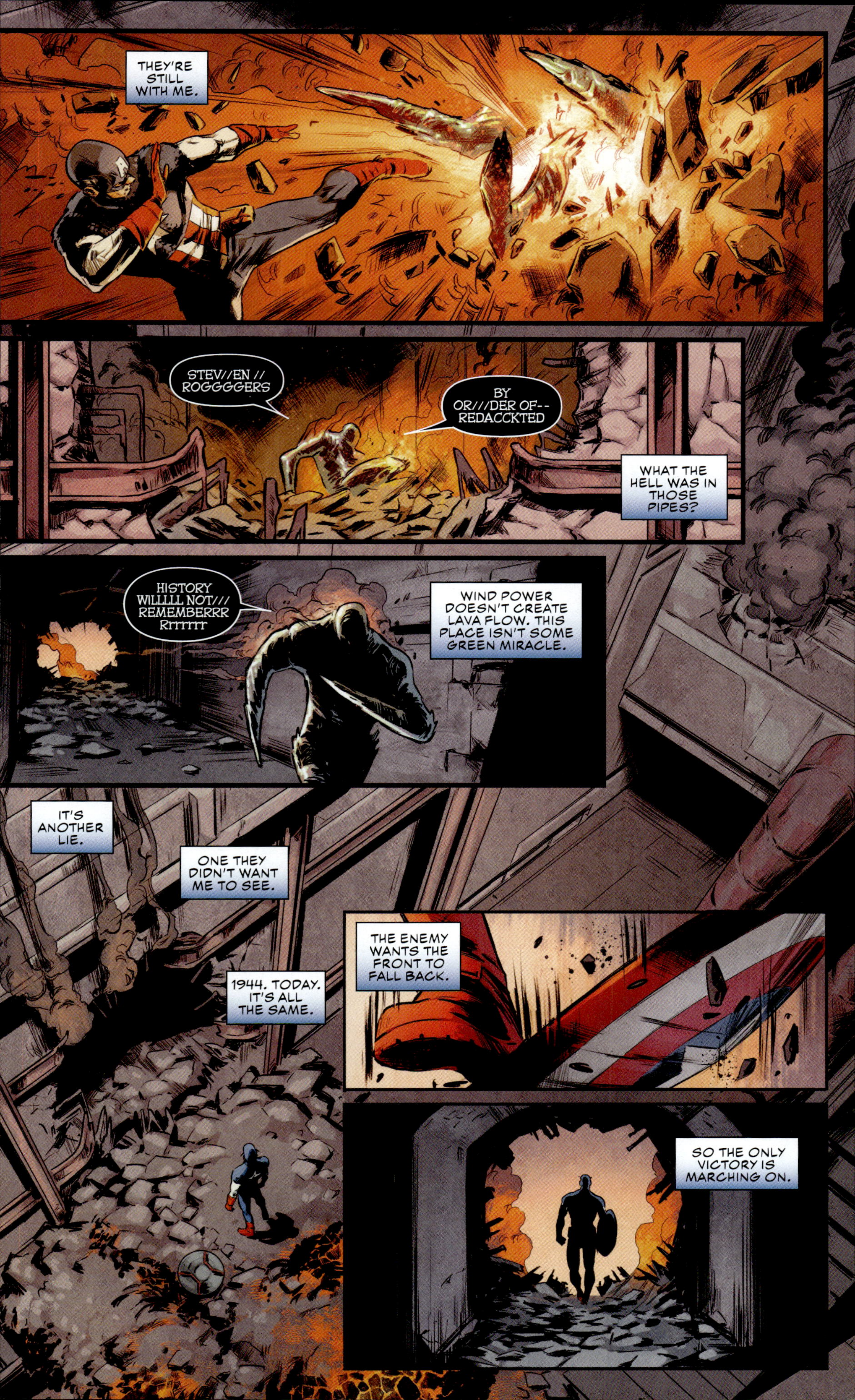
THEY'RE STILL WITH ME.
STEV//EN // ROGGGGERS
BY OR///DER OF-- REDACCKTED
WHAT THE HELL WAS IN THOSE PIPES?
HISTORY WILLLLL NOT/// REMEMBERRR Rrrrrrr
WIND POWER DOESN'T CREATE LAVA FLOW. THIS PLACE ISN'T SOME GREEN MIRACLE.
IT'S ANOTHER LIE.
ONE THEY DIDN'T WANT ME TO SEE.
1944. TODAY. IT'S ALL THE SAME.
THE ENEMY WANTS THE FRONT TO FALL BACK.
SO THE ONLY VICTORY IS MARCHING ON.

THE DAY KING T'CHAKA PASSED ALONG THE VIBRANIUM THAT WOULD BECOME MY SHIELD...
...HE PASSED ALONG TWO PIECES OF WISDOM I'LL NEVER FORGET.
"THE METAL IS YOUR PROTECTOR. RESPECT IT."
THAT WAS THE FIRST. THE SECOND I WOULDN'T UNDERSTAND FOR YEARS TO COME.
"THE METAL IS YOUR TEACHER," T'CHAKA TOLD ME.
THRUMMMMMMMMM
"LISTEN TO IT."
THIS MACHINE, THIS...*REDACTED.* IT THINKS IT HAS ME IN ITS TRAP.
IT CAN'T HEAR THE SURGING, BOUNDLESS POWER UNDER OUR FEET.
BUT MY TEACHER CAN.

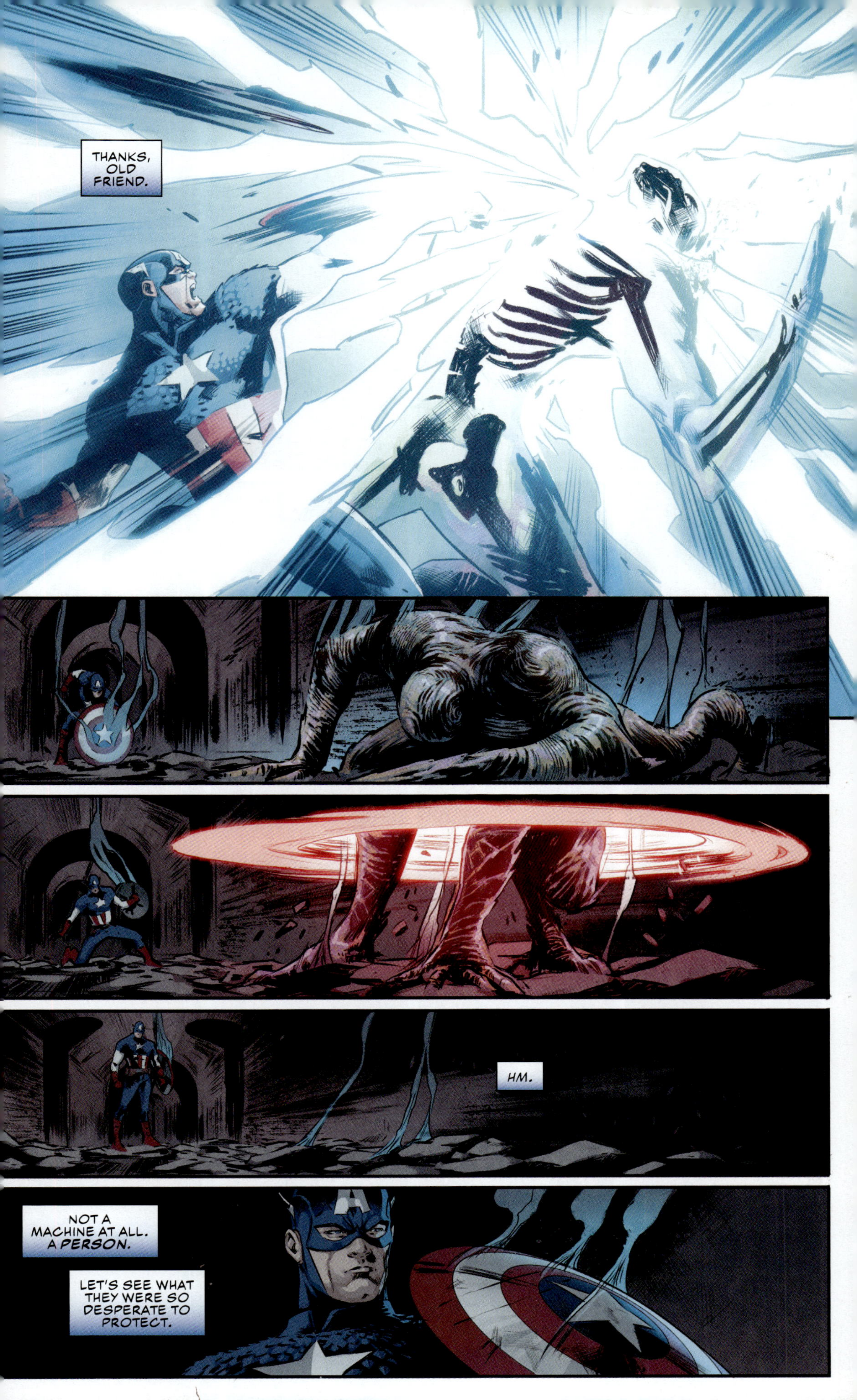
THANKS, OLD FRIEND.
HM.
NOT A MACHINE AT ALL. A PERSON.
LET'S SEE WHAT THEY WERE SO DESPERATE TO PROTECT.

FORGE
RESTRICTED
IT'S NOT THE *FACILITY* THEY WANTED.

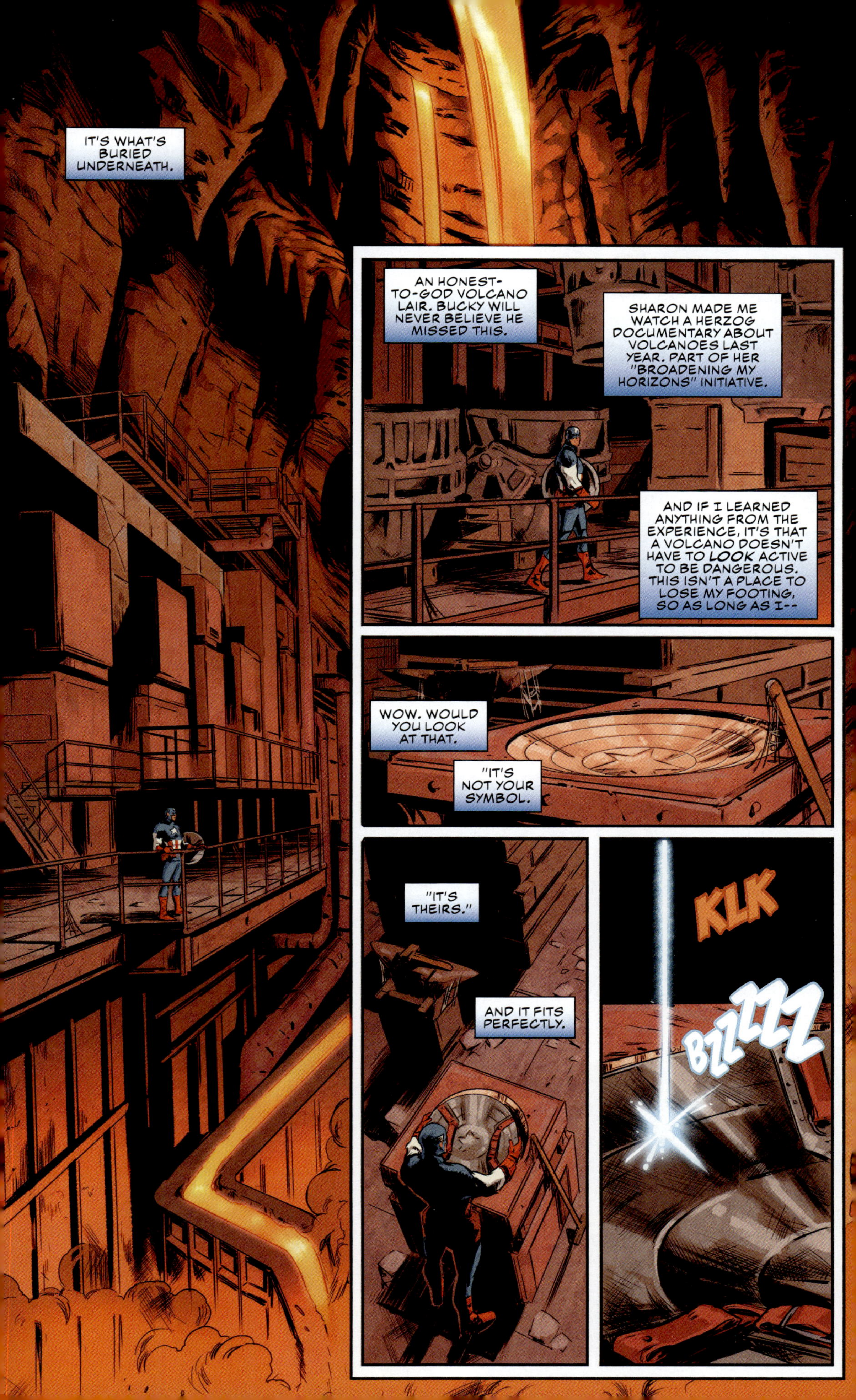
IT'S WHAT'S BURIED UNDERNEATH.
AN HONEST-TO-GOD VOLCANO LAIR. BUCKY WILL NEVER BELIEVE HE MISSED THIS.
SHARON MADE ME WATCH A HERZOG DOCUMENTARY ABOUT VOLCANOES LAST YEAR. PART OF HER "BROADENING MY HORIZONS" INITIATIVE.
AND IF I LEARNED ANYTHING FROM THE EXPERIENCE, IT'S THAT A VOLCANO DOESN'T HAVE TO LOOK ACTIVE TO BE DANGEROUS. THIS ISN'T A PLACE TO LOSE MY FOOTING, SO AS LONG AS I--
WOW. WOULD YOU LOOK AT THAT.
"IT'S NOT YOUR SYMBOL.
"IT'S THEIRS."
AND IT FITS PERFECTLY.
KLK
BZZZZZ

PRIVATE ROGERS.
MY NAME IS DR. BOKA AGBOJE. BY THE TIME YOU HEAR THIS, I WILL EITHER BE DEAD OR I WILL HAVE SUCCESSFULLY DISAPPEARED. IN EITHER CASE, BY HEARING THIS MESSAGE, YOU HAVE COMPLETED YOUR MISSION--JUST AS I HAVE COMPLETED MINE.
I WAS TASKED BY MY GOVERNMENT IN AGREEMENT WITH THE U.S. ARMY TO CONSTRUCT AND OPERATE THIS VIBRANIUM ALLOY FORGE. IT IS HERE THAT YOUR PROMISED SHIELD HAS BEEN CREATED.
EXCEPT THIS PLACE IS NOT RUN BY YOUR UNITED STATES.
IT'S YOURS.
TAKE THE SHIELD. IT'S NOT THEIRS ANYMORE.
I AM HOPING YOU ARE THE MAN I THINK YOU ARE. THE MAN YOU THINK YOU ARE.
THE KIND OF MAN WHO FIGHTS FOR FREEDOM. FOR THE WORLD. FOR THE PEOPLE. FOR HIMSELF, MOST OF ALL.

THEY'RE CALLED THE OUTER CIRCLE. THEY SURROUND EVERYTHING. THEY INFLUENCE EVERYTHING.
OUR WORLD IS THEIR GAME.
THEIR SYMBOL IS THREE RINGS AROUND A STAR. AN OUTER CIRCLE THAT CONTROLS. TWO INNER CIRCLES THAT OBEY. AND A STAR--THEIR WEAPON OF ENFORCEMENT. THEIR SUPER-SOLDIER.
THEY THINK THIS SYMBOL WILL REMAIN HIDDEN. BUT WITH THE ONLY ADVANCED METAL IN THEIR ARSENAL, I HAVE BROUGHT IT PERMANENTLY INTO THE LIGHT.
YOU, STEVE ROGERS. YOU ARE THEIR STAR. YOU WILL WIELD THIS SHIELD, AND I AM HOPING AGAINST HOPE THAT PAWN IS NOT A ROLE YOU WILL ACCEPT.
THEY HAVE ORCHESTRATED THIS WAR. FOR THE LAST TWENTY YEARS, HUMANKIND HAS LIVED UNDER THEIR SHADOW. AND IF ALLOWED TO DO SO, THEY SHALL PLAY A GAME WITH THE ENTIRE CENTURY.

CAPTAIN AMERICA.
NEARLY A CENTURY LATER...
...AND YOU STILL DON'T KNOW YOUR PLACE.
YOU MUST BE THE MACHINE. HERE TO "SECURE THE FORGE."
I OWE YOU NO EXPLANATION.
EXCEPT YOU DIDN'T COME HERE FOR THE POWER. THAT'S NOT WHY YOU SENT YOUR SOLDIER AFTER ME.
YOU WANTED TO KEEP ME FROM HEARING THAT MESSAGE. AND YOU FAILED.
INDEED.
FORTUNATELY, A BETTER MOVE HAS PRESENTED ITSELF.
BIP

BIP
BIP
BIP
BIP
BIP
BOOM
"I HOPE YOU'RE THE MAN YOU THINK YOU ARE."
BIP
AND YOU ARE. YOU REALLY ARE.
MY SON WAS AN EXCELLENT JUDGE OF CHARACTER.
IT GOT HIM KILLED AS WELL.
BIP
BIP
BOOM
GOODBYE, CAPTAIN AMERICA. I CAN REBUILD A POWER PLANT...

NO ONE CAN REBUILD YOU.

"I THINK I'M DONE PLAYING CARDS, MR. BARNES."

IT DOESN'T HAVE TO GO LIKE THIS.
YES. I COULD BELIEVE YOU.
ABOUT MY ENTIRE LIFE BEING A LIE.
ADMIT MYSELF TO BE ONE OF THE GREAT FOOLS OF THE TWENTIETH CENTURY.
AFRAID I'M GOING TO PASS.
THERE ARE PROBABLY A LOT OF TOUGH GUYS IN THIS ROOM. WAITING TO SEE WHICH WAY THIS CONVERSATION IS GOING TO BREAK. I'VE GOT TO APPLAUD YOU ALL FOR THE RESTRAINT.
BUT IF YOU KNOW WHO WE ARE...AND EVEN IF YOU DON'T, I SUGGEST YOU GET OUT.
NOW.
PEGGY. I HAVE PROOF.
SAVE IT. I DIDN'T FIND YOU CHARMING BEFORE YOUR DEFECTION. I DON'T FIND YOU TERRIBLY SYMPATHETIC NOW. SO WHEN YOU CALL ME A LIAR, A PUPPET AND A SECRET FASCIST...
...I'M AFRAID I TAKE THAT RATHER PERSONALLY.

BAM
TCHK
BAM
BAM
TCHK
TCHK
PEGGY, STAND DOWN! I'M NOT YOUR ENEMY!
NOT HOW THIS WORKS, JAMES.
YOU'RE GUILTY. YOU'VE DONE TERRIBLE THINGS AND PRETENDED FOR A LONG TIME THAT IT WASN'T REALLY YOU.
BUT IT WAS, SOLDAT.
AND I'LL NOT BE DRAGGED INTO YOUR TRAGEDY!

CONSIDER THIS YOUR FINAL WARNING TO STAY THE HELL OUT OF MY BUSINESS, BARNES!
SHINK
CRACK
THRUNK
AND IF I WAS ON THE TAKE, YOU'D BE DEAD RIGHT NOW.
DON'T LOOK FOR ME.
DON'T THINK ABOUT ME.
WIPE MY NAME FROM YOUR IMAGINATION.

I'M NOT LYING TO YOU!
I'M TRYING TO WAKE YOU UP.
UNLESS YOU ALREADY KNOW YOU'RE ON THE TAKE, IN WHICH CASE--
OH, PLEASE DO SHUT UP.
IF YOU REALLY BELIEVE IS NONSENSE, YOU'RE RISK TO ANYONE AND EVERYONE AROUND YOU.
IF WHAT YOU'RE SAYING IS REAL, I'LL FIND OUT FOR MYSELF. AND I'LL BRING THEM MY JUSTICE.
BUT YOU, WINTER SOLDIER?
YOU'LL NEVER SEE ME AGAIN.

MORTIMER STREET BOXING
"STEVEN ROGERS
"BY ORDER OF THE OUTER CIRCLE"
NO PAIN NO GAIN
YOU HAVE BEEN REDACTED
HISTORY WILL NOT REMEMBER YOU

SKOTTIE YOUNG

CAPTAIN AMERICA: SENTINEL OF LIBERTY #1 VARIANT

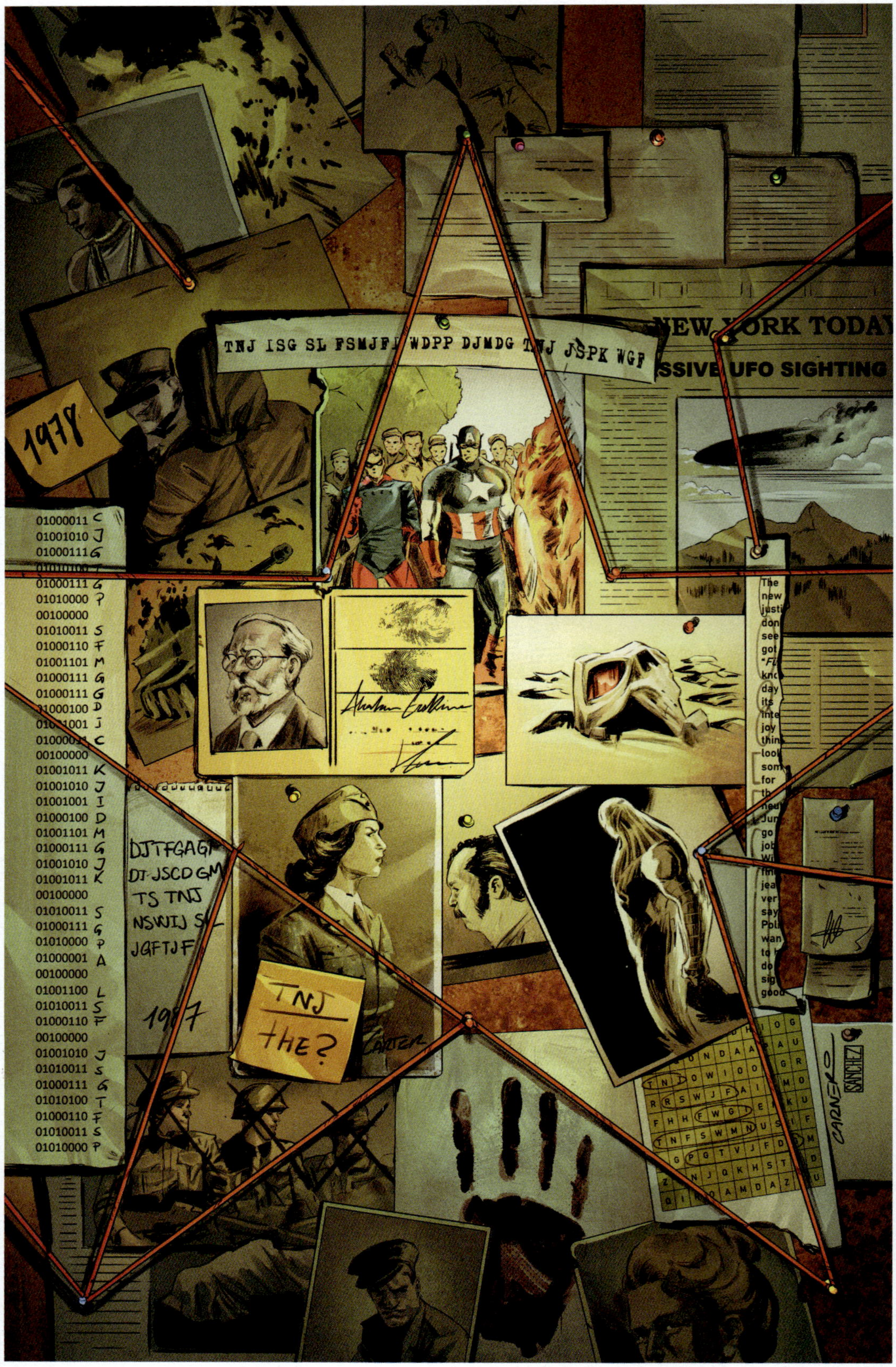

CAPTAIN AMERICA: SENTINEL OF LIBERTY #4

EVERYTHING IN ITS RIGHT PLACE.

WHEN I WAS A KID ON THESE STREETS, MY MOM WOULD SAY THOSE WORDS A LOT.
WHEN SHE WANTED ME TO CLEAN MY ROOM, WHEN SHE FINISHED A PUZZLE ON THE KITCHEN TABLE, WHEN SHE LEARNED SOME NEW FACT THAT CHANGED THE WAY SHE LOOKED AT THE WORLD.
WHEN EINSTEIN CRACKED RELATIVITY. WHEN PHINEAS HORTON REVEALED HIS HUMAN TORCH. WHEN FDR DECLARED WAR.
"GOD'S PLAN."
BUT IN THE THREE SLEEPLESS DAYS SINCE HEARING THE MESSAGE LEFT ON MY SHIELD NEARLY A CENTURY AGO...SINCE SEEING THE OUTER CIRCLE IN ACTION... I'VE ONLY BEEN ABLE TO WONDER.
415
WAS IT GOD'S PLAN MY MOTHER SPENT HER LIFE FULFILLING? THAT I SPENT MY LIFE UPHOLDING?
OR WAS IT *THEIRS?*
"THE FURTHER I LOOK, THE LESS I FIND."

SEE WHAT I MEAN, ALPINE? THE FISK FILE* WAS ONE THING, BUT MOST OF THESE OLD REPORTS ARE REDACTED SO MUCH, THE PAPER MIGHT AS WELL BE BLACK.
BROO?
IF YOU'VE GOT SOME CLEVER ESPIONAGE SKILLS YOU'VE BEEN HIDING, NOW WOULD BE THE TIME. OR MAYBE YOU COULD BE THE VERY BEST CAT AND GO DOWN TO THE BODEGA, PICK ME UP SOME MORE ASPIRIN--
KNOCK KNOCK KNOCK
*FROM DEVIL'S REIGN: WINTER SOLDIER #1!
COUNT OF THREE. I GO FOR THE GUT, YOU GO FOR THE FACE.
THREE...
TWO...
HEY, BUCK. YOU CAN TELL THE CAT TO STAND DOWN.
YOU LOOK LIKE HELL, BY THE WAY.
LONG COUPLE NIGHTS.
WE BOTH KNOW THAT'S A HALF-TRUTH AT BEST.
STEVE...
TOO MANY SECRETS BETWEEN US, BUCK.
I THINK IT'S TIME WE HAD A TALK.

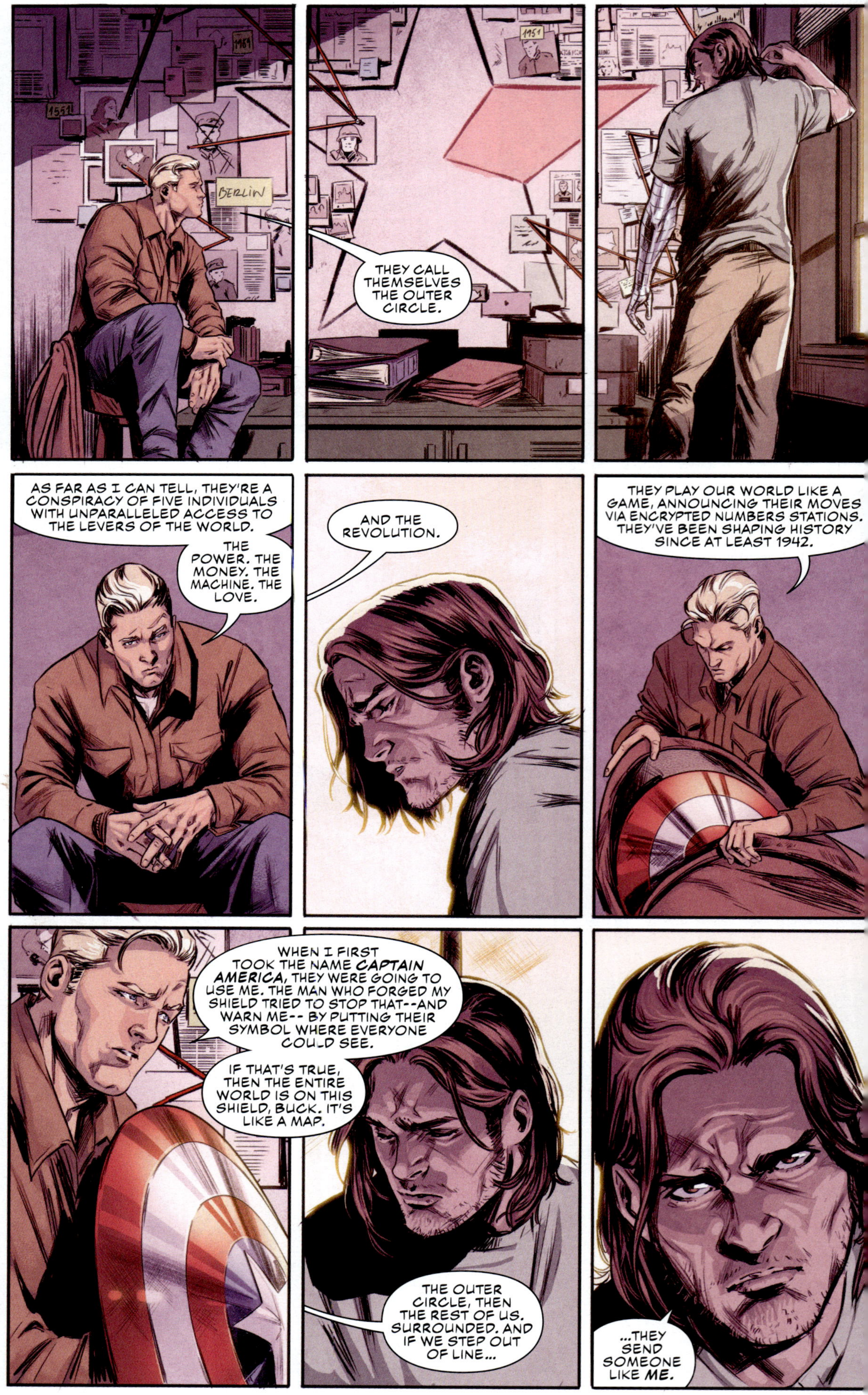
BERLIN
1984
1951
THEY CALL THEMSELVES THE OUTER CIRCLE.
AS FAR AS I CAN TELL, THEY'RE A CONSPIRACY OF FIVE INDIVIDUALS WITH UNPARALLELED ACCESS TO THE LEVERS OF THE WORLD.
THE POWER. THE MONEY. THE MACHINE. THE LOVE.
AND THE REVOLUTION.
THEY PLAY OUR WORLD LIKE A GAME, ANNOUNCING THEIR MOVES VIA ENCRYPTED NUMBERS STATIONS. THEY'VE BEEN SHAPING HISTORY SINCE AT LEAST 1942.
WHEN I FIRST TOOK THE NAME ***CAPTAIN AMERICA***, THEY WERE GOING TO USE ME. THE MAN WHO FORGED MY SHIELD TRIED TO STOP THAT--AND WARN ME-- BY PUTTING THEIR SYMBOL WHERE EVERYONE COULD SEE.
IF THAT'S TRUE, THEN THE ENTIRE WORLD IS ON THIS SHIELD, BUCK. IT'S LIKE A MAP.
THE OUTER CIRCLE, THEN THE REST OF US. SURROUNDED. AND IF WE STEP OUT OF LINE...
...THEY SEND SOMEONE LIKE ***ME***.

THEY CALL US STARPOINTS.
FIVE ASSASSINS THEY USE TO MAKE SURE HISTORY PLAYS OUT THE WAY THEY CHOOSE.
LIKE THAT NEW DESTROYER WE WENT UP AGAINST ON THE FOURTH.
HE CALLED ME SOMETHING. BEFORE THEY FLIPPED HIS SWITCH.
"THE GREAT *CENTURY WEAPON*."
I'VE KNOWN FOR A FEW MONTHS. THOUGHT IT WAS JUST ANOTHER LAYER TO THE WINTER SOLDIER'S... TO *MY* GOD-AWFUL LEGACY.
MORE BLOOD ON MY HANDS. ANOTHER HUNT FOR PEACE.
I DIDN'T KNOW ABOUT THE CIRCLE. I DIDN'T WANT TO...DRAG YOU INTO THIS.
I... STEVE...
...I THOUGHT I WAS ALONE IN THIS.
BUCKY.
YOU'VE BEEN MY BEST FRIEND FOR EIGHTY YEARS.
THOUGHT YOU WOULD'VE LEARNED BY NOW.

YOU NEVER FIGHT ALONE.
1951

WE MAKE A PLAN. PUT TOGETHER A WAY TO TAKE THE FIGHT TO THEM.
WE SWEAR TO DO IT TOGETHER.
HOW COULD WE NOT?
BUT LIKE ANYTHING WORTH DOING, THE PLAN'S NOT WITHOUT A FAIR SHARE OF RISK.
THANK YOU FOR WALKING AMARI TO SCHOOL, MISTER ROG--I MEAN, STEVE!
YOU'RE MY SECOND-FAVORITE CAPTAIN AMERICA!
OF COURSE, DANIELA! AND NO WORRIES, SAM'S MY FAVORITE TOO!
EVERY WORD HAS TO BE PERFECT. EVERY MOVE MADE CAREFULLY.
EXCITED TO GO BACK TO SCHOOL, KIDDO?
YEAH...
...ESPECIALLY 'CUZ I GOT MY HAYMAKER DOWN NOW.
I CAN'T WAIT TO SHOW THOSE BULLIES WHAT'S UP.
EVERYTHING IN ITS RIGHT PLACE.
AMARI, LISTEN TO ME.

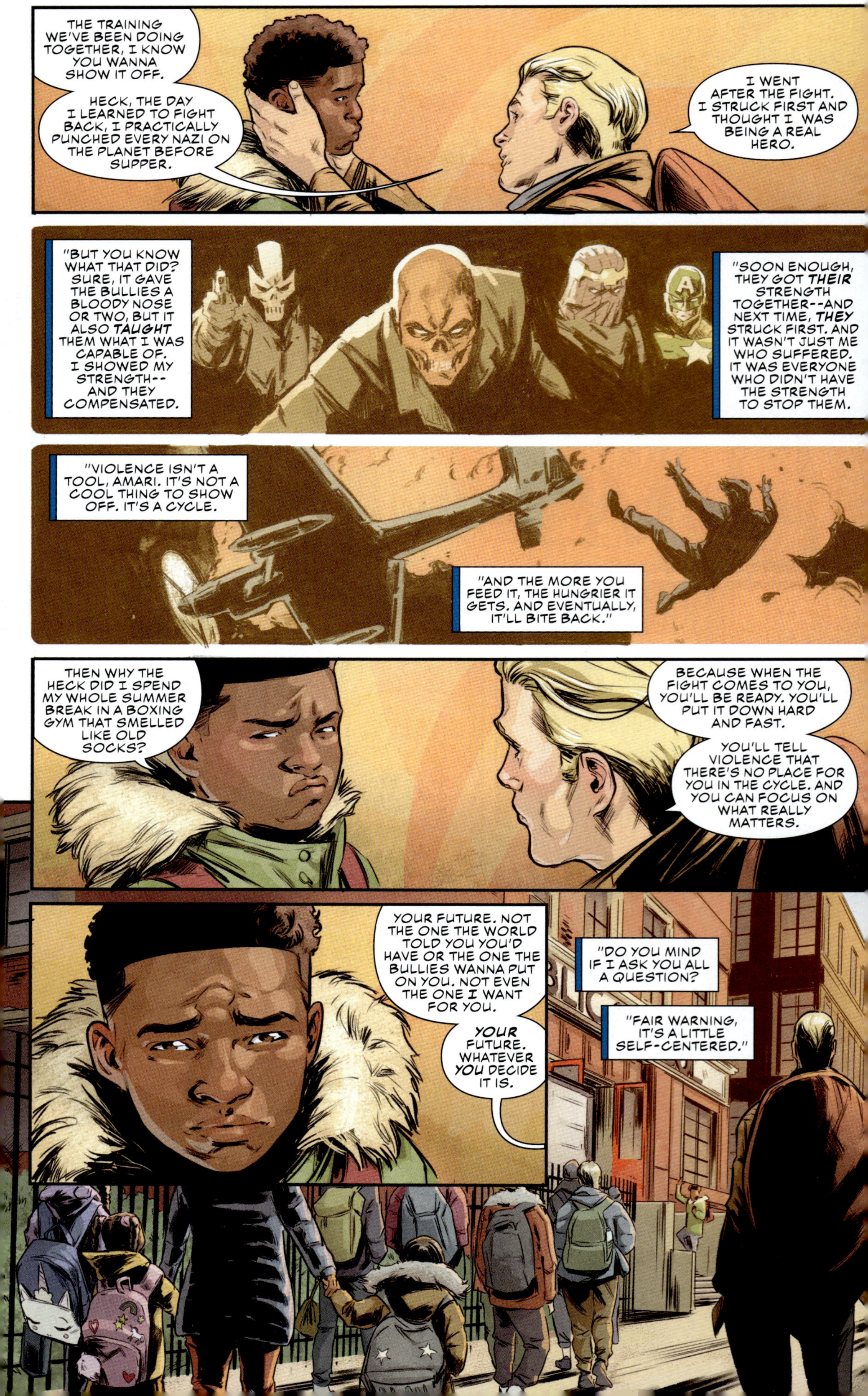
THE TRAINING WE'VE BEEN DOING TOGETHER, I KNOW YOU WANNA SHOW IT OFF.
HECK, THE DAY I LEARNED TO FIGHT BACK, I PRACTICALLY PUNCHED EVERY NAZI ON THE PLANET BEFORE SUPPER.
I WENT AFTER THE FIGHT. I STRUCK FIRST AND THOUGHT I WAS BEING A REAL HERO.
"BUT YOU KNOW WHAT THAT DID? SURE, IT GAVE THE BULLIES A BLOODY NOSE OR TWO, BUT IT ALSO *TAUGHT* THEM WHAT I WAS CAPABLE OF. I SHOWED MY STRENGTH-- AND THEY COMPENSATED.
"SOON ENOUGH, THEY GOT *THEIR* STRENGTH TOGETHER--AND NEXT TIME, *THEY* STRUCK FIRST. AND IT WASN'T JUST ME WHO SUFFERED. IT WAS EVERYONE WHO DIDN'T HAVE THE STRENGTH TO STOP THEM.
"VIOLENCE ISN'T A TOOL, AMARI. IT'S NOT A COOL THING TO SHOW OFF. IT'S A CYCLE.
"AND THE MORE YOU FEED IT, THE HUNGRIER IT GETS. AND EVENTUALLY, IT'LL BITE BACK."
THEN WHY THE HECK DID I SPEND MY WHOLE SUMMER BREAK IN A BOXING GYM THAT SMELLED LIKE OLD SOCKS?
BECAUSE WHEN THE FIGHT COMES TO YOU, YOU'LL BE READY. YOU'LL PUT IT DOWN HARD AND FAST.
YOU'LL TELL VIOLENCE THAT THERE'S NO PLACE FOR YOU IN THE CYCLE. AND YOU CAN FOCUS ON WHAT REALLY MATTERS.
YOUR FUTURE. NOT THE ONE THE WORLD TOLD YOU YOU'D HAVE OR THE ONE THE BULLIES WANNA PUT ON YOU. NOT EVEN THE ONE *I* WANT FOR YOU.
YOUR FUTURE. WHATEVER *YOU* DECIDE IT IS.
"DO YOU MIND IF I ASK YOU ALL A QUESTION?
"FAIR WARNING, IT'S A LITTLE SELF-CENTERED."

WHAT DOES THE SHIELD MEAN TO YOU?
YOU MEAN, BESIDES BEING A REAL SON OF A BITCH TO RENDER PROPERLY?
I MEAN, IT MEANS **AMERICA.** RIGHT? THE STARS AND STRIPES FOREVER, YANKEE-DOODLE DANDY--
LEFT AND RIGHT, RED, WHITE AND BLUE, I GET MINE, YOU GET YOURS, DON'T TREAD ON ME NONSENSE.
SO IT'S A SYMBOL OF CORRUPTION.
AND INJUSTICE, SURE. BUT ALSO HOPE.
IT SAYS HELP IS ON THE WAY.
IT'S A COMFORTING SMILE.
MIA! YOU REALLY GONNA BAD-MOUTH THE AMERICAN DREAM IN FRONT OF STEVE? MIGHT AS WELL SLAP HIS MAMA WHILE YOU'RE AT IT.
OH WHATEVER, STEVE KNOWS--HE'S BEEN FIGHTING WHITE SUPREMACISTS LONGER THAN WE'VE BEEN ALIVE.
YEAH. LIKE THAT ONE RIGHT THERE.
BUT COME ON, MAN. YOU'VE SPENT A CENTURY CARRYING THAT THING. YOU KNOW HOW MUCH IT MEANS TO FOLKS.
I THINK THE REAL QUESTION HERE, STEVE-O...
...IS WHAT DOES THE SHIELD MEAN TO *YOU?*

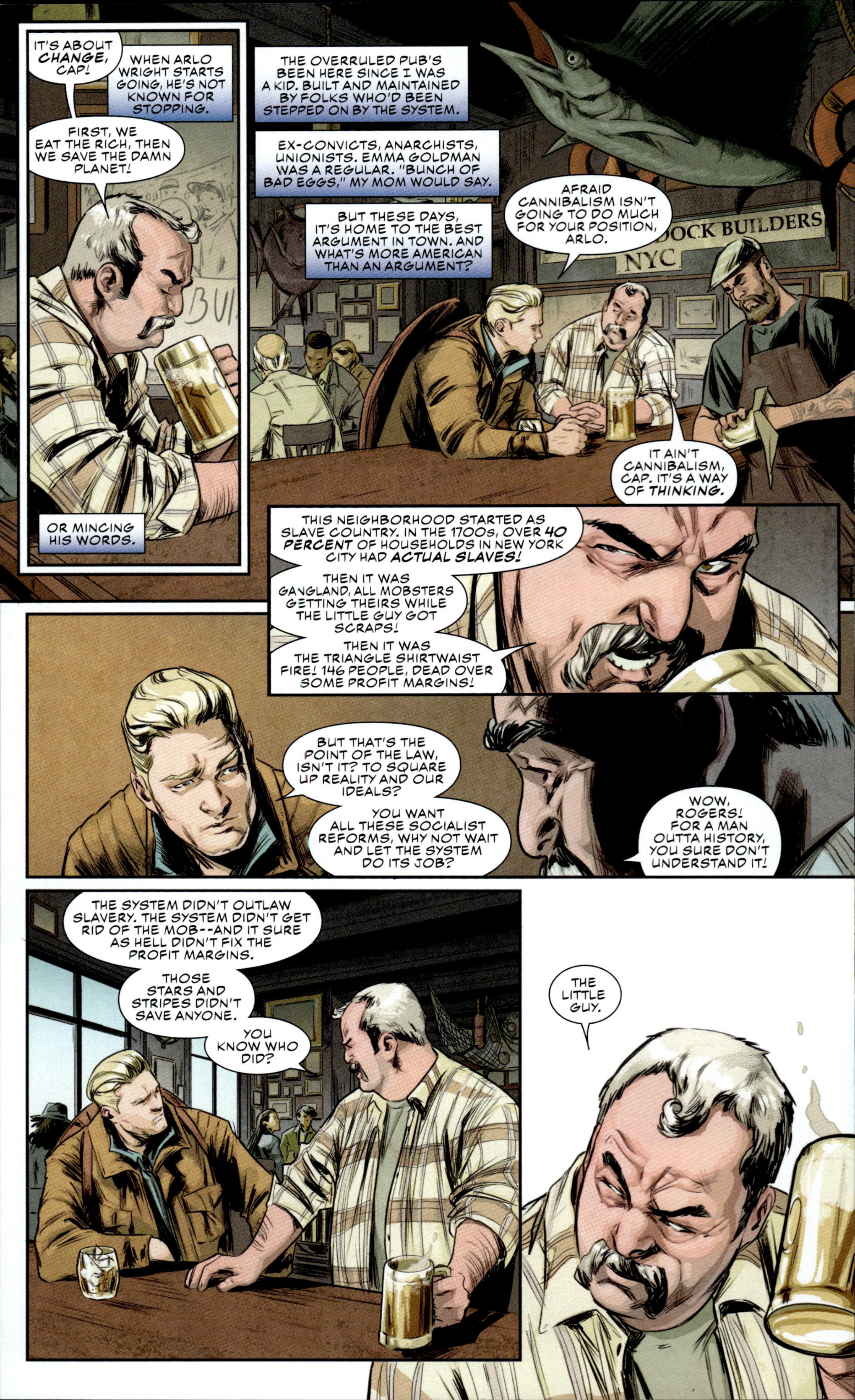
IT'S ABOUT CHANGE, CAP!
WHEN ARLO WRIGHT STARTS GOING, HE'S NOT KNOWN FOR STOPPING.
FIRST, WE EAT THE RICH, THEN WE SAVE THE DAMN PLANET!
OR MINCING HIS WORDS.
THE OVERRULED PUB'S BEEN HERE SINCE I WAS A KID. BUILT AND MAINTAINED BY FOLKS WHO'D BEEN STEPPED ON BY THE SYSTEM.
EX-CONVICTS, ANARCHISTS, UNIONISTS. EMMA GOLDMAN WAS A REGULAR. "BUNCH OF BAD EGGS," MY MOM WOULD SAY.
BUT THESE DAYS, IT'S HOME TO THE BEST ARGUMENT IN TOWN. AND WHAT'S MORE AMERICAN THAN AN ARGUMENT?
AFRAID CANNIBALISM ISN'T GOING TO DO MUCH FOR YOUR POSITION, ARLO.
DOCK BUILDERS
NYC
IT AIN'T CANNIBALISM, CAP. IT'S A WAY OF THINKING.
THIS NEIGHBORHOOD STARTED AS SLAVE COUNTRY. IN THE 1700S, OVER 40 PERCENT OF HOUSEHOLDS IN NEW YORK CITY HAD ACTUAL SLAVES!
THEN IT WAS GANGLAND, ALL MOBSTERS GETTING THEIRS WHILE THE LITTLE GUY GOT SCRAPS!
THEN IT WAS THE TRIANGLE SHIRTWAIST FIRE! 146 PEOPLE, DEAD OVER SOME PROFIT MARGINS!
BUT THAT'S THE POINT OF THE LAW, ISN'T IT? TO SQUARE UP REALITY AND OUR IDEALS?
YOU WANT ALL THESE SOCIALIST REFORMS, WHY NOT WAIT AND LET THE SYSTEM DO ITS JOB?
WOW, ROGERS! FOR A MAN OUTTA HISTORY, YOU SURE DON'T UNDERSTAND IT!
THE SYSTEM DIDN'T OUTLAW SLAVERY. THE SYSTEM DIDN'T GET RID OF THE MOB--AND IT SURE AS HELL DIDN'T FIX THE PROFIT MARGINS.
THOSE STARS AND STRIPES DIDN'T SAVE ANYONE.
YOU KNOW WHO DID?
THE LITTLE GUY.

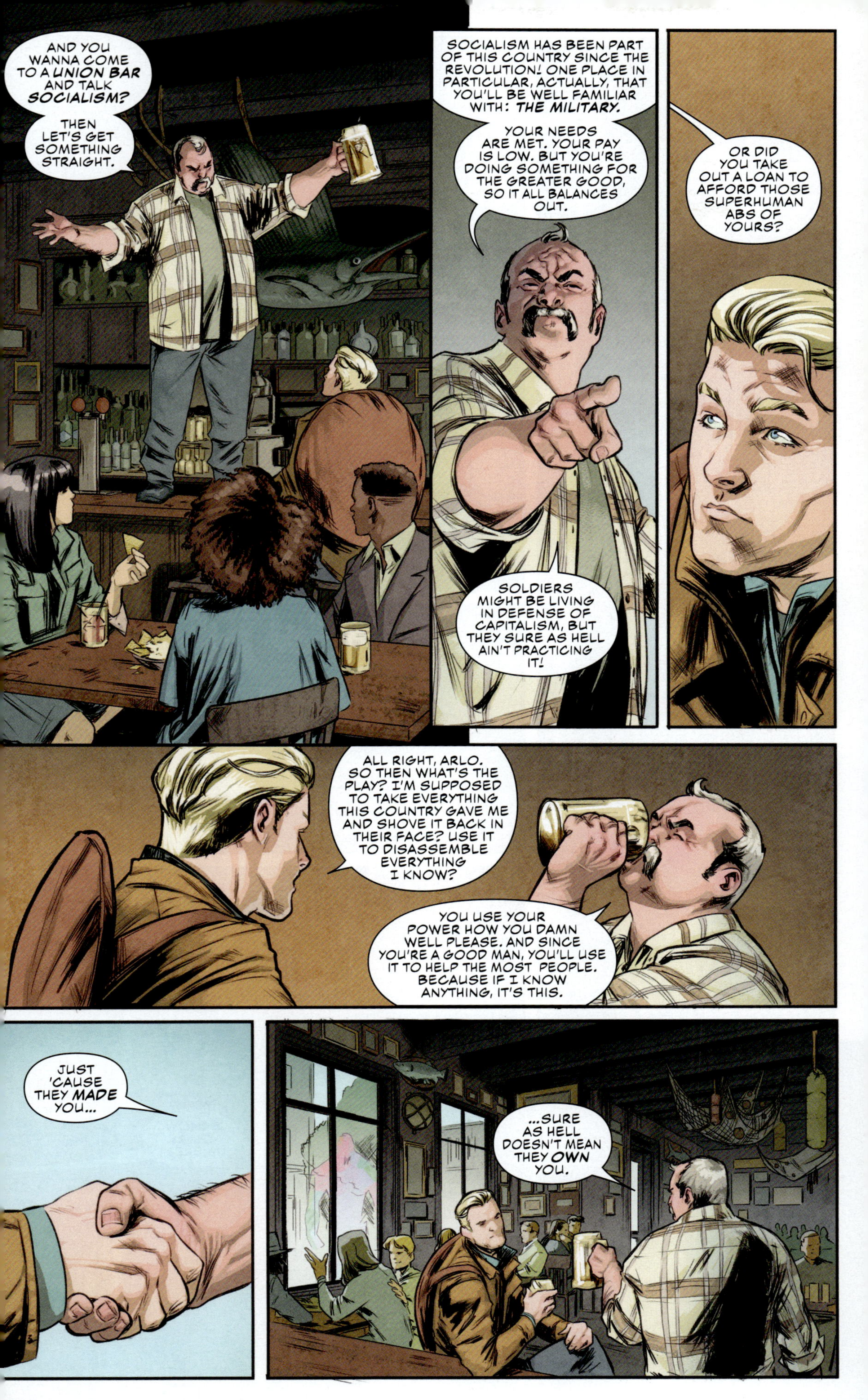
AND YOU WANNA COME TO A UNION BAR AND TALK SOCIALISM?
THEN LET'S GET SOMETHING STRAIGHT.
SOCIALISM HAS BEEN PART OF THIS COUNTRY SINCE THE REVOLUTION! ONE PLACE IN PARTICULAR, ACTUALLY, THAT YOU'LL BE WELL FAMILIAR WITH: THE MILITARY.
YOUR NEEDS ARE MET. YOUR PAY IS LOW. BUT YOU'RE DOING SOMETHING FOR THE GREATER GOOD, SO IT ALL BALANCES OUT.
SOLDIERS MIGHT BE LIVING IN DEFENSE OF CAPITALISM, BUT THEY SURE AS HELL AIN'T PRACTICING IT!
OR DID YOU TAKE OUT A LOAN TO AFFORD THOSE SUPERHUMAN ABS OF YOURS?
ALL RIGHT, ARLO. SO THEN WHAT'S THE PLAY? I'M SUPPOSED TO TAKE EVERYTHING THIS COUNTRY GAVE ME AND SHOVE IT BACK IN THEIR FACE? USE IT TO DISASSEMBLE EVERYTHING I KNOW?
YOU USE YOUR POWER HOW YOU DAMN WELL PLEASE. AND SINCE YOU'RE A GOOD MAN, YOU'LL USE IT TO HELP THE MOST PEOPLE. BECAUSE IF I KNOW ANYTHING, IT'S THIS.
JUST 'CAUSE THEY MADE YOU...
...SURE AS HELL DOESN'T MEAN THEY OWN YOU.

I KNOW YOU'RE THERE.

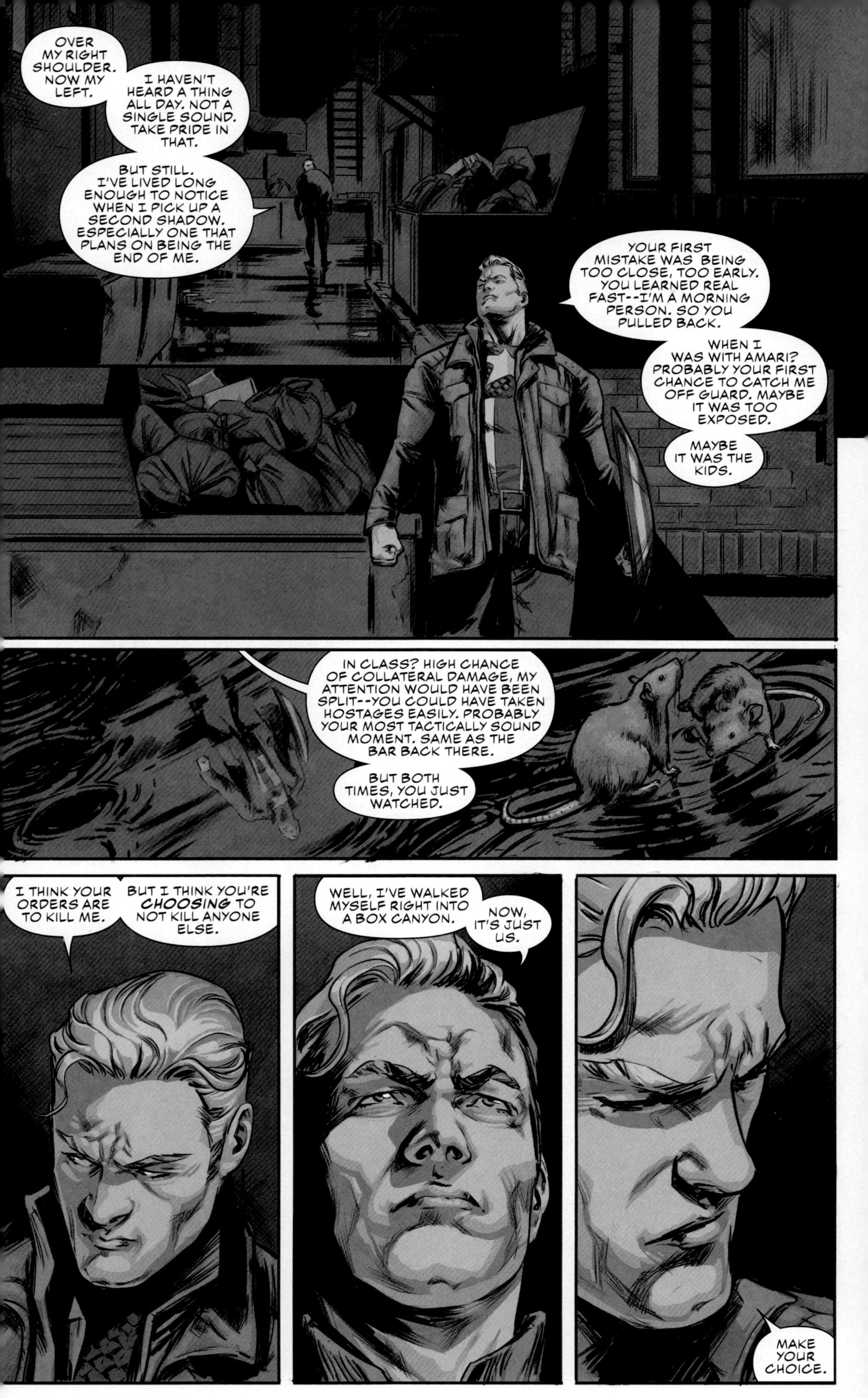
OVER MY RIGHT SHOULDER. NOW MY LEFT.
I HAVEN'T HEARD A THING ALL DAY. NOT A SINGLE SOUND. TAKE PRIDE IN THAT.
BUT STILL. I'VE LIVED LONG ENOUGH TO NOTICE WHEN I PICK UP A SECOND SHADOW. ESPECIALLY ONE THAT PLANS ON BEING THE END OF ME.
YOUR FIRST MISTAKE WAS BEING TOO CLOSE, TOO EARLY. YOU LEARNED REAL FAST--I'M A MORNING PERSON. SO YOU PULLED BACK.
WHEN I WAS WITH AMARI? PROBABLY YOUR FIRST CHANCE TO CATCH ME OFF GUARD. MAYBE IT WAS TOO EXPOSED.
MAYBE IT WAS THE KIDS.
IN CLASS? HIGH CHANCE OF COLLATERAL DAMAGE, MY ATTENTION WOULD HAVE BEEN SPLIT--YOU COULD HAVE TAKEN HOSTAGES EASILY. PROBABLY YOUR MOST TACTICALLY SOUND MOMENT. SAME AS THE BAR BACK THERE.
BUT BOTH TIMES, YOU JUST WATCHED.
I THINK YOUR ORDERS ARE TO KILL ME.
BUT I THINK YOU'RE *CHOOSING* TO NOT KILL ANYONE ELSE.
WELL, I'VE WALKED MYSELF RIGHT INTO A BOX CANYON.
NOW, IT'S JUST US.
MAKE YOUR CHOICE.

STEVEN ROGERS. YOU WILL BE REDACTED!
THOSE ARE YOUR ORDERS. CAN'T ARGUE WITH THAT.
BUT I ALSO KNOW THAT YOU HAVEN'T JUST BEEN FOLLOWING ME...
TRONK
...YOU'VE BEEN LISTENING TO EVERY WORD I'VE SAID.

SKRAFTCH!
YOU WILL BE FORGOTTEN!
WELL, SOLDIER, I HOPE YOU WERE PAYING ATTENTION...
...SINCE I'VE BEEN TALKING TO YOU THE WHOLE TIME.

"EVERYTHING IN ITS RIGHT PLACE."
THAT'S WHAT MY MOM USED TO TELL ME. AND IT MAKES SENSE FOR KIDS WITH MESSY TOY BOXES.
THE PROBLEM STARTS WHEN THE REST OF THE WORLD STARTS SAYING IT TOO.
BECAUSE THE IDEA DOESN'T SCALE. YOU HAVE ENOUGH POWER, YOU HAVE EVERYTHING. YOUR MESSY TOY BOX BECOMES THE WHOLE DAMN WORLD.
PUBLIC SCH
YOUR FUTURE. WHATEVER *YOU* DECIDE IT IS.
EXCEPT YOU'RE NOT A THING, ARE YOU?
YOU'RE NOT A MONSTER OR A MACHINE. I SAW A PERSON UNDER THERE IN GERMANY. I KNOW YOU'RE MORE THAN THEIR WEAPON. AND I KNOW THAT YOU THINK THE CIRCLE IS YOUR LIFE.
THE LITTLE GUY.
"EVERYONE WHO LAUGHS AND THINKS AND LIVES INSIDE THE CIRCLE."

AND BELIEVE IT OR NOT, YOU'RE CHOOSING TO FOLLOW THEM.
WHAT DOES THE SHIELD MEAN TO YOU?
THAT'S WHAT THEY DON'T UNDERSTAND ABOUT US.
ALL OF US.
WE CAN CHOOSE OUR PLACE.

YOU MAY HAVE TO FIGHT FOR IT.
AND IT MIGHT NOT BE PERFECT.
BUT IF WE HAVE EACH OTHER'S BACKS, YOU CAN STAND FREE.
I DON'T KNOW--WHO YOU ARE OR *HOW* YOU--HAPPENED.
BUT, SOLDIER, AFTER TODAY, YOU HAVE A *CLEAR* IDEA ABOUT ME.
SO LET ME ASK YOU, FOR MAYBE THE FIRST TIME:
WHAT PLACE DO YOU CHOOSE?

I'M GOING TO THEM. WHEREVER THEY ARE.
THEY'RE PLAYING A GAME. METICULOUS. PRECISE.
I'M GOING TO FLIP THE TABLE.
WANT TO HELP?

Starpoint R
Status:
Offline.
WHO WOULD HAVE THOUGHT IT'D HAPPEN SO SOON?
THE REVOLUTION CALLS THE TABLE TO CONVENE.
AND PREPARE A MOVE FOR BROADCAST.
REVOLUTION.
CAPTAIN AMERICA TO THE SHADOW CAPITOL.
FINAL MOVE.

CARMEN CARNERO & ALEJANDRO SÁNCHEZ

CAPTAIN AMERICA: SENTINEL OF LIBERTY #1 2ND PRINTING VARIANT

CAPTAIN AMERICA: SENTINEL OF LIBERTY #5

SO. YOU FINALLY DID IT.
YOU BROUGHT ROGERS TO THE CAPITOL. YOU BURNED IT ALL DOWN.
BUT ONLY YOU WILL GET CAUGHT IN THE FIRE.
YOU WANT TO STOP PLAYING?
FINE.
I'M DONE TRYING TO WIN THE GAME BY YOUR RULES.
REVOLUTION, Y HEART, THINK OF THE LONG GAME.
THAT'S THE POINT ENTIRELY, LOVE. THE GAME'S TOO LONG.
WHEN I'M GONE, WATCH THE VIDEO ON THIS DRIVE. WITH MY LOVE.
MHHM. MYSTERIOUS.
BUT I'LL NOT WEEP FOR YOU...
OH, SPARE ME.
ALL YOU KNOW IS FAILURE, REVOLUTION. I AM UNSURPRISED THAT IT'S WHAT YOU PREDICT.
YOU ALWAYS DID GO OFF HALF-COCKED--EVER SINCE THAT DRUNKEN NIGHT ON FRANZ JOSEPH STREET. BUT THIS IS JUVENILE, EVEN FOR YOU.

"...NOR THOSE WHO GET KILLED IN YOUR NAME."
THAT'S 38,000 FEET AND CLIMBING, WITHOUT A HITCH IN HER STEP. YOU WERE RIGHT--SHE'S OLD, BUT DAMN WELL BUILT.
JUST THIS, BUCKY.
WE'RE IN THIS TOGETHER.
NO MATTER HOW BAD IT GETS DOWN THERE... I'LL BACK YOUR PLAY.

THE FREEDOM'S FLIGHT ISN'T OLD, CAPTAIN MERRICK. SHE'S CLASSIC.
EITHER WAY, CAPTAIN, I'M GLAD YOU CALLED. HAVE SHIELD, WILL TRAVEL. ANY TIME, ANYWHERE.
BUT YOU SURE THIS SHADOW CAPITOL IS DOWN THERE? A GIANT SHIELD-SHAPED AIRSHIP IS HARD TO MISS, AND RADAR'S READING NOTHING BUT AIR UNTIL THE SPLAT ZONE.
TRUST ME, IT'S THERE. INTEL'S GOOD.
I TRUST MY SOURCES.
ONCE THE PLAN STARTS, WE'RE RADIO SILENT. ANYONE HAVE ANY LAST WORDS?
HERE.
NOW.
BWEE BWEE BWEE
THAT'S OUR CUE...

DECEMBER OF '44, I SAW THE TEETH OF HELL.
LET'S FLY.
TWENTY MILES OF FROZEN FRONT LINE DESIGNED FOR ONE PURPOSE.
DEATH.

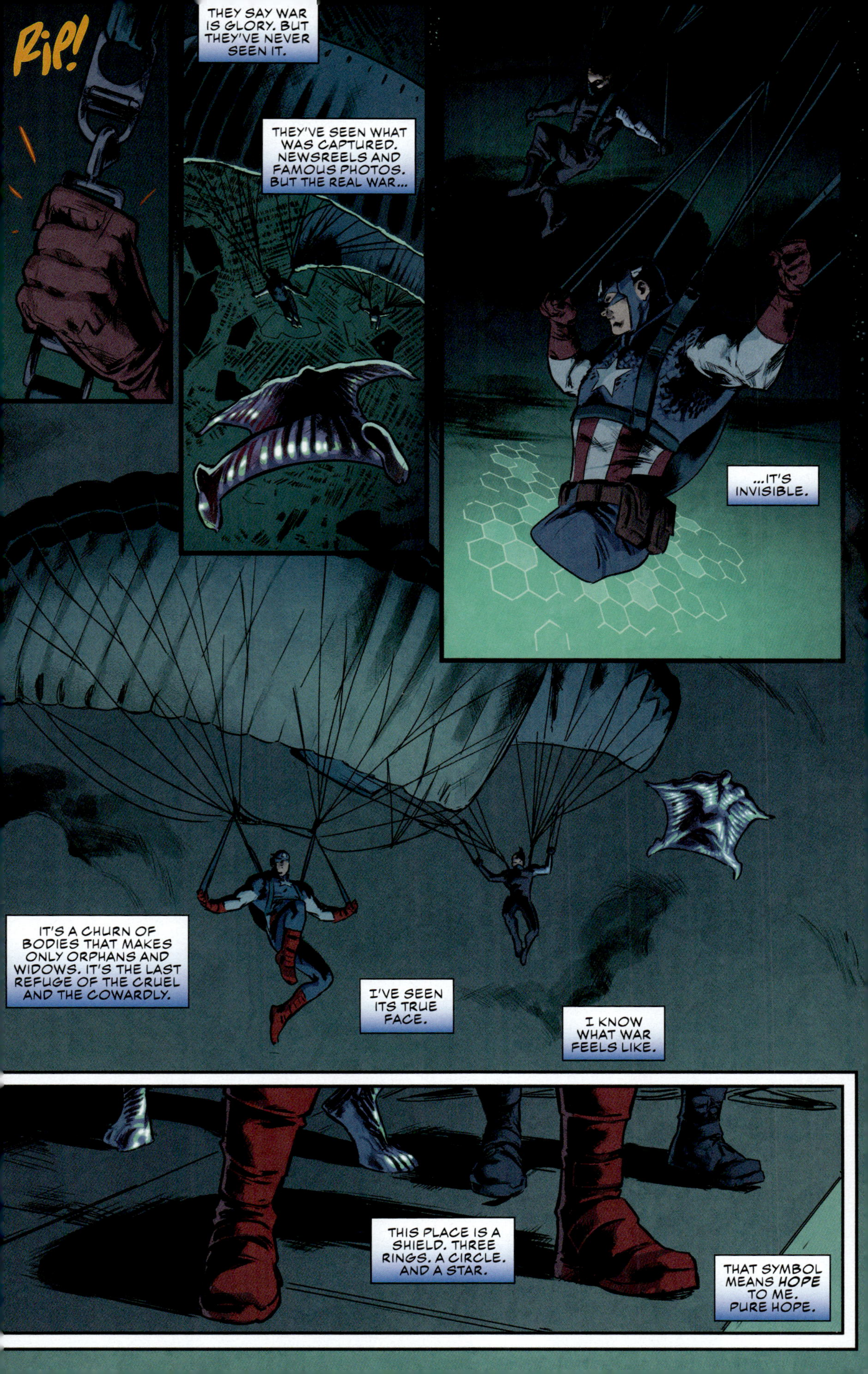
RIP!
THEY SAY WAR IS GLORY. BUT THEY'VE NEVER SEEN IT.
THEY'VE SEEN WHAT WAS CAPTURED. NEWSREELS AND FAMOUS PHOTOS. BUT THE REAL WAR...
...IT'S INVISIBLE.
IT'S A CHURN OF BODIES THAT MAKES ONLY ORPHANS AND WIDOWS. IT'S THE LAST REFUGE OF THE CRUEL AND THE COWARDLY.
I'VE SEEN ITS TRUE FACE.
I KNOW WHAT WAR FEELS LIKE.
THIS PLACE IS A SHIELD. THREE RINGS. A CIRCLE. AND A STAR.
THAT SYMBOL MEANS *HOPE* TO ME. PURE HOPE.

BUT HERE, IT JUST MEANS WAR.

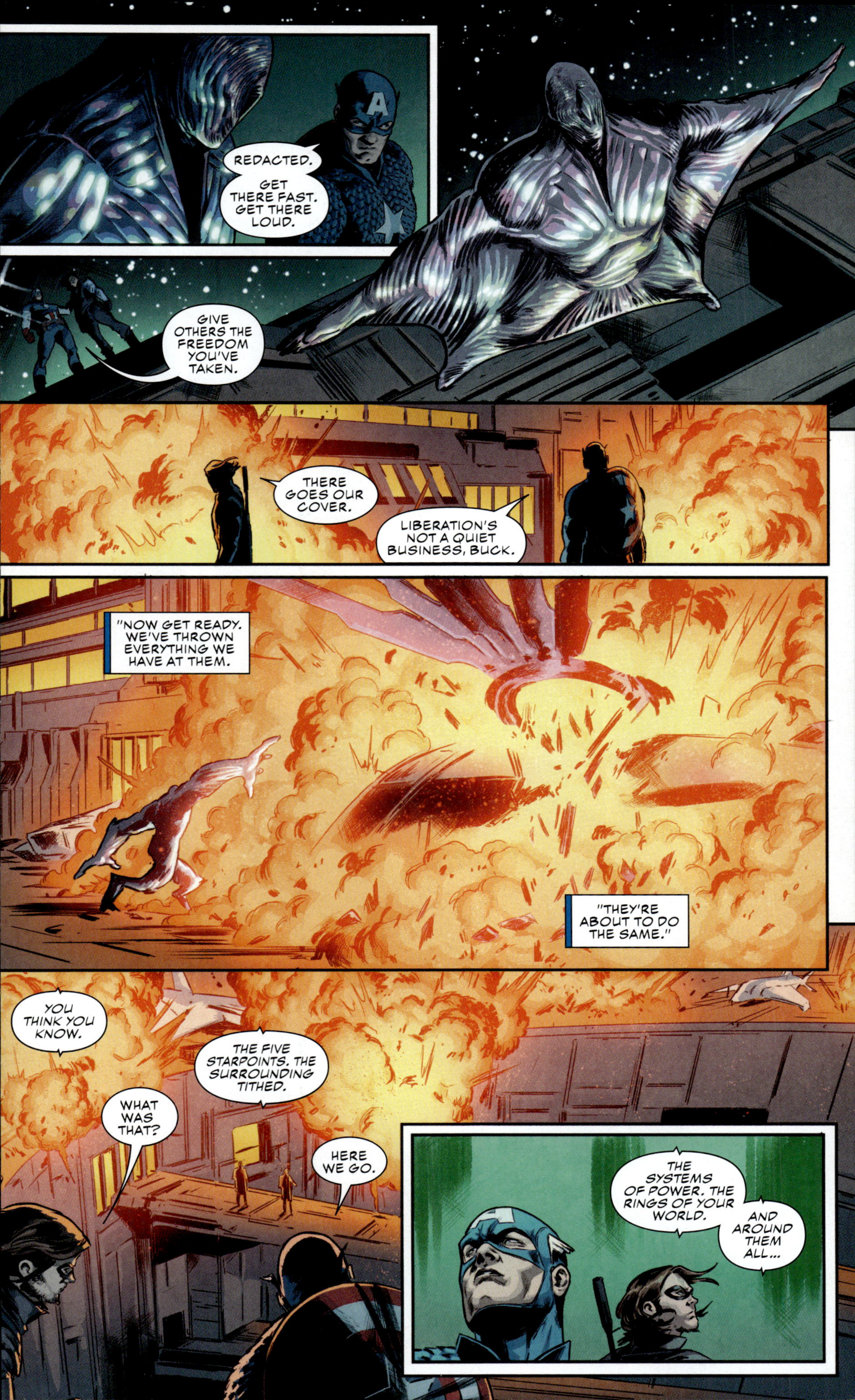
REDACTED.
GET THERE FAST. GET THERE LOUD.
GIVE OTHERS THE FREEDOM YOU'VE TAKEN.
THERE GOES OUR COVER.
LIBERATION'S NOT A QUIET BUSINESS, BUCK.
"NOW GET READY. WE'VE THROWN EVERYTHING WE HAVE AT THEM.
"THEY'RE ABOUT TO DO THE SAME."
YOU THINK YOU KNOW.
THE FIVE STARPOINTS. THE SURROUNDING TITHED.
WHAT WAS THAT?
HERE WE GO.
THE SYSTEMS OF POWER. THE RINGS OF YOUR WORLD.
AND AROUND THEM ALL...

...AN OUTER CIRCLE.

THE MONEY. THE POWER. THE LOVE. THE REVOLUTION. AND, OF COURSE, MYSELF. THE MACHINE.
YOU'VE BEEN TRACKING OUR MOVES, A SPECTATOR TO THE ONLY GAME THAT MATTERS. OUR CENTURY GAME.
AGENTS OF CHAOS. YET YOU THINK US MONSTERS.
NO. WE'RE THE SURVIVORS.
AT THE BIRTH OF THE CENTURY, THE WORLD PAINTED ITSELF IN BLOOD AND BONE. WE ARE THE CHILDREN OF THAT ARMAGEDDON.
AND SO WE GREW WITH THE MILLENNIUM, TO WEAVE THE STORY OF THE WORLD. WITH EVERY STRAND OF SONG AND SECRET WISH. AND YES, WITH TRAGEDY.
WE DON'T CONTROL. WE INSPIRE.
WE BEND THE WORLD.
AND THOSE WHO KNOW-- NOT THE LEADERS, BUT THOSE IN TRUE POWER-- THEY UNDERSTAND. THAT'S WHY THEY TITHE. SOLDIERS, EQUIPMENT, ALL TOOLS IN OUR BELT. THE WHOLE DAMNED WORLD, LOYAL TO THE CIRCLE.
THE GAME FOR THE TWENTIETH CENTURY ENDED IN A DRAW. BECAUSE WE WERE ALL SO COOPERATIVE--THE MONEY, THE MACHINE AND MYSELF.
BECAUSE CHAOS IS INFINITELY WORSE. IT IS INHUMANE. IT IS INTOLERABLE.
A CENTURY WHERE MEN LIKE YOU COULD GROW INTO ICONS. BUT IT HAS BECOME TEDIOUS.
THE GAME FOR THE TWENTY-FIRST HAS JUST BEGUN.
THE POWER.
MOVE 23.
CAPTAIN AMERICA DIES.

TITHED. ON YOUR LIVES.
ATTACK.
JUST FOLLOW THE PLAN.
THIS WASN'T PART OF THE PLAN.
SURE IT WAS, BUCK.
THIS IS THE PART WHERE WE WIN.

THESE SOLDIERS CAME FROM EVERYWHERE. FROM EVERYONE.
THEY COULD HAVE BEEN US. THEY PRACTICALLY ARE.
NO KILLING.
THAT'S THE RULE AND WE BOTH KNOW IT.
RULES ARE HARDEST TO KEEP WHEN THE BULLETS START FLYING, THOUGH.
I CAN FEEL IT IN MY GUT. THAT TIGER IN BUCKY'S TRIGGER FINGER.
THE WAY HE HOLDS IT BACK AMAZES ME. ALWAYS HAS.

BUT HE'S GOT LIMITS THAT DON'T HOLD WITHOUT HELP.
WE HAVE A HORDE INCOMING. THAT'S IT. I'M OPENING UP.
NO.
NOT ANOTHER STEP.
I WILL SHOOT YOU. I CAN'T...
THEY WON'T LET ME PUT THE GUN DOWN.
KA-CLICK!
I KNOW. THOSE SUITS ARE RIGGED TO EXPLODE IF YOU DISOBEY. TIED TO AN IMPENETRABLE CENTRAL SERVER. BUT TRUST ME...
...YOU CAN PUT THAT GUN DOWN.
ALL YOU HAVE TO DO IS TRY.

KA-CHUNK
IT DIDN'T WORK.
IT DOESN'T WORK! THE BOMBS, THEY'RE-- THE TRIGGER, IT'S OFFLINE SOMEHOW!
PAOLO, GET UP. IT'S OKAY.
WHAT...WHAT HAPPENED?
I DON'T KNOW HOW HE DID IT...
...BUT I THINK WE JUST GOT SAVED BY CAPTAIN AMERICA.
YOU SAVED YOURSELF. AND AS FOR DEACTIVATING THE BOMBS IN YOUR SUITS...

"...YOU'VE GOT SOMEONE ELSE TO THANK FOR THAT."
WHAT'S YOUR NAME?
...ARMITAGE. STACI ARMITAGE. MI:13.
GET THE OTHERS OUT OF HERE, STACI.
YES, SIR.
PLEASE.
CALL ME STEVE.

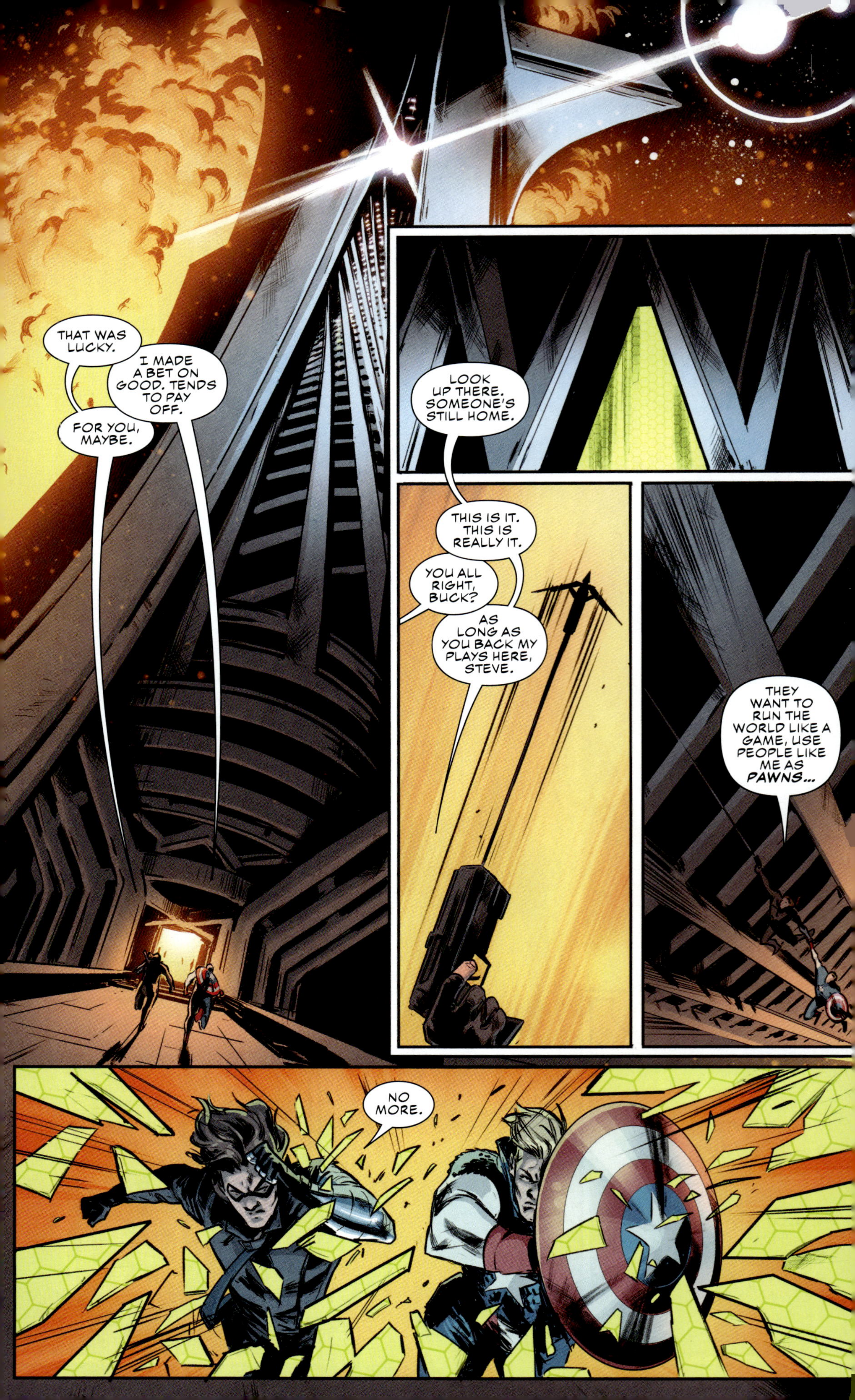
THAT WAS LUCKY.
I MADE A BET ON GOOD. TENDS TO PAY OFF.
FOR YOU, MAYBE.
LOOK UP THERE. SOMEONE'S STILL HOME.
THIS IS IT. THIS IS REALLY IT.
YOU ALL RIGHT, BUCK?
AS LONG AS YOU BACK MY PLAYS HERE, STEVE.
THEY WANT TO RUN THE WORLD LIKE A GAME, USE PEOPLE LIKE ME AS PAWNS...
NO MORE.

CLAP CLAP CLAP
HELLO, MR. BARNES.
SORRY ABOUT THE LIGHTS. YOU JUST MISSED THE OTHERS. THEY GAVE THAT OMINOUS SPEECH AND WENT TO GROUND.
POWER MAKES COWARDS OF US ALL.
BUT HONESTLY, BETWEEN YOU AND ME, I'M THE ONLY ONE WHO MATTERS. AND I'VE BEEN WAITING SO LONG TO HAVE THIS CONVERSATION.
YOU WERE USED. YOU WERE DISCARDED. YOU WERE SAVED. YOU WERE USED AGAIN. AND ALL OF IT DONE SO IMPERSONALLY. A TACTIC INFUSED BY ITS VERY NATURE WITH SHAME.
WHY, I HAD TO INVOLVE STEVE ROGERS-- THE MOST DANGEROUS PAWN ON THE BOARD--JUST TO GET YOU HERE. SUCH SECRECY.
LET'S SHED SOME LIGHT, SHALL WE?
YOU CAN CALL ME THE REVOLUTION.
YOU'VE WORKED FOR ME YOUR ENTIRE LIFE, JAMES.
YOU WANT LIBERTY? TRUE LIBERTY?
GO AHEAD.
TAKE IT.
IT'S YOURS.

THE HELL ARE YOU PLAYING AT? WHO ARE YOU REALLY?
STEVE. NO. MY MISSION, REMEMBER? MY CALL.
BUCKY, WE CAN'T PLAY HIS GAME.
IT'S NOT A CHOICE, ROGERS. JAMES KNOWS THAT. HE'S HAD PLENTY OF EXPERIENCE ON THE BOARD.
WHAT HE DOESN'T KNOW IS THAT HE CAN SIT AT THE TABLE.
AND ALL HE HAS TO DO IS WHAT HE CAME HERE TO DO.
WE DIDN'T COME HERE TO KILL YOU.
STEVE.
YOU SHOULD GO.

YOU GOT ONE THING WRONG, REVOLUTION.
I DON'T NEED YOUR LITTLE PISTOL.
I BROUGHT MY OWN.
BUCKY, STOP. THINK ABOUT THIS.
IT'S ALL I'VE THOUGHT ABOUT FOR MONTHS, STEVE. I'VE READ THE FILE. I KNOW EVERYTHING.
THEY PICKED ME WHEN I WAS A KID. THEY SET UP MY DAD TO DIE. THEY GOT ME ADOPTED BY THE DAMN ARMY. ALL SO I COULD KILL FOR THEM. RIGHT NEXT TO YOU.
ALL SO I COULD HELP THEM CONTROL YOU. AND WHEN THAT DIDN'T WORK...THEY PULLED THE STRINGS TO MAKE ME THE WINTER SOLDIER.
A PAST COVERED IN BLOOD. A SIN I CAN'T EVER WASH OUT.
BUT IT'S NOT MY SIN.
IT'S THEIRS.

YOU'RE NOT GONNA PULL THAT TRIGGER, BUCKY.
BUCK...
STEVE. GET OUT OF THE WAY.
DAMMIT, STEVE, GET OUT OF MY WAY!
I'M NOT IN YOUR WAY, BUCK!
YOU ARE.
DON'T GIVE IN TO VENGEANCE.

THIS ISN'T VENGEANCE, STEVE.
IT'S A REVOLUTION.
BUCKY, WAIT--

PEACH MOMOKO

CAPTAIN AMERICA: SENTINEL OF LIBERTY #2 VARIANT

CAPTAIN AMERICA: SENTINEL OF LIBERTY #6

THIS ISN'T HAPPENING.
MY MIND KNOWS THE PAIN OF A BULLET.
WHAT IT'S LIKE TO DIE ON THE FLOOR WITH SURPRISE IN YOUR EYES.
I KNOW THIS FEELING. I KNOW IT'S REAL.
BUT I STILL CAN'T BELIEVE IT.
THE TRIGGER'S PULLED. THE DAMAGE IS DONE. BUCKY'S FALLEN INTO THEIR TRAP.
BUT THIS MOMENT IS WHAT I MAKE IT...

...AND I DON'T HAVE TO LET THIS HAPPEN.
STAY DOWN, STEVE. I'LL CALL OFF THE ALARMS, GET YOU MEDICAL ATTENTION.
IF WHAT THE REVOLUTION SAID WAS TRUE... I HAVE POWER IN THIS PLACE NOW.
BLAM
BLAM
YOU DON'T KNOW THAT, BUCKY. YOU DON'T...KNOW ANYTHING RIGHT NOW. YOU JUST KILLED A MAN.
YOUR MIND'S... FLOODED WITH... REVENGE.
BUT YOU STILL KNOW ENOUGH...TO SHOOT FOR THE SHOULDER.
YOU'LL HAVE TO BRAG TO SHARON NEXT TIME WE'RE ALL TOGETHER.
DAMMIT, STEVE. DON'T YOU DARE.
IT'S OKAY, BUCKY.

YOU GOT WHAT YOU CAME FOR.
NOW LET'S GET OUT OF HERE.
TOGETHER.
BECAUSE MAKE NO MISTAKE, EVEN WITH A BAD SHOULDER...
...I'M STILL STRONG ENOUGH TO DRAG YOU THE HELL BACK HOME.
KLIK!
CLATTER
STEVE. YOU GOTTA LISTEN TO ME.
BECAUSE I'M ONLY GONNA SAY THIS ONCE.

THE OUTER CIRCLE TOOK EVERYTHING FROM ME. BEFORE I EVEN KNEW I HAD IT.
THAT MAN, THE REVOLUTION, HAD POWER NEITHER OF US CAN EVEN DREAM OF. AND HE KNEW, HE KNEW, WHAT KIND OF MONSTER IT HAD TURNED HIM INTO.
THIS ISN'T A PROBLEM YOU CAN PUNCH. IT'S NOT A PROBLEM YOU CAN TALK DOWN. THIS SYSTEM HAS HELD FOR A CENTURY, AND IT'S NOT GONNA BREAK BECAUSE YOU PLANT YOURSELF LIKE A TREE.
THINGS LIKE THIS ONLY GET DESTROYED FROM WITHIN.
I HAVE A PLAN. IT'S GOING TO WORK.
BUT NOT IF YOU'RE STANDING OVER MY SHOULDER. UNDERSTAND?
I GO WHERE YOU CAN'T. IT'S ALWAYS BEEN THAT WAY. SINCE LEHIGH.
SO UNTIL THIS PLACE IS BURNED TO THE GROUND...
...THIS IS WHERE I BELONG.
I'M NOT LEAVING YOU BEHIND, BUCKY. NEVER AGAIN.
AND I'M NOT LEAVING THIS PLACE, STEVE.

THEN THERE'S NOTHING LEFT TO SAY.

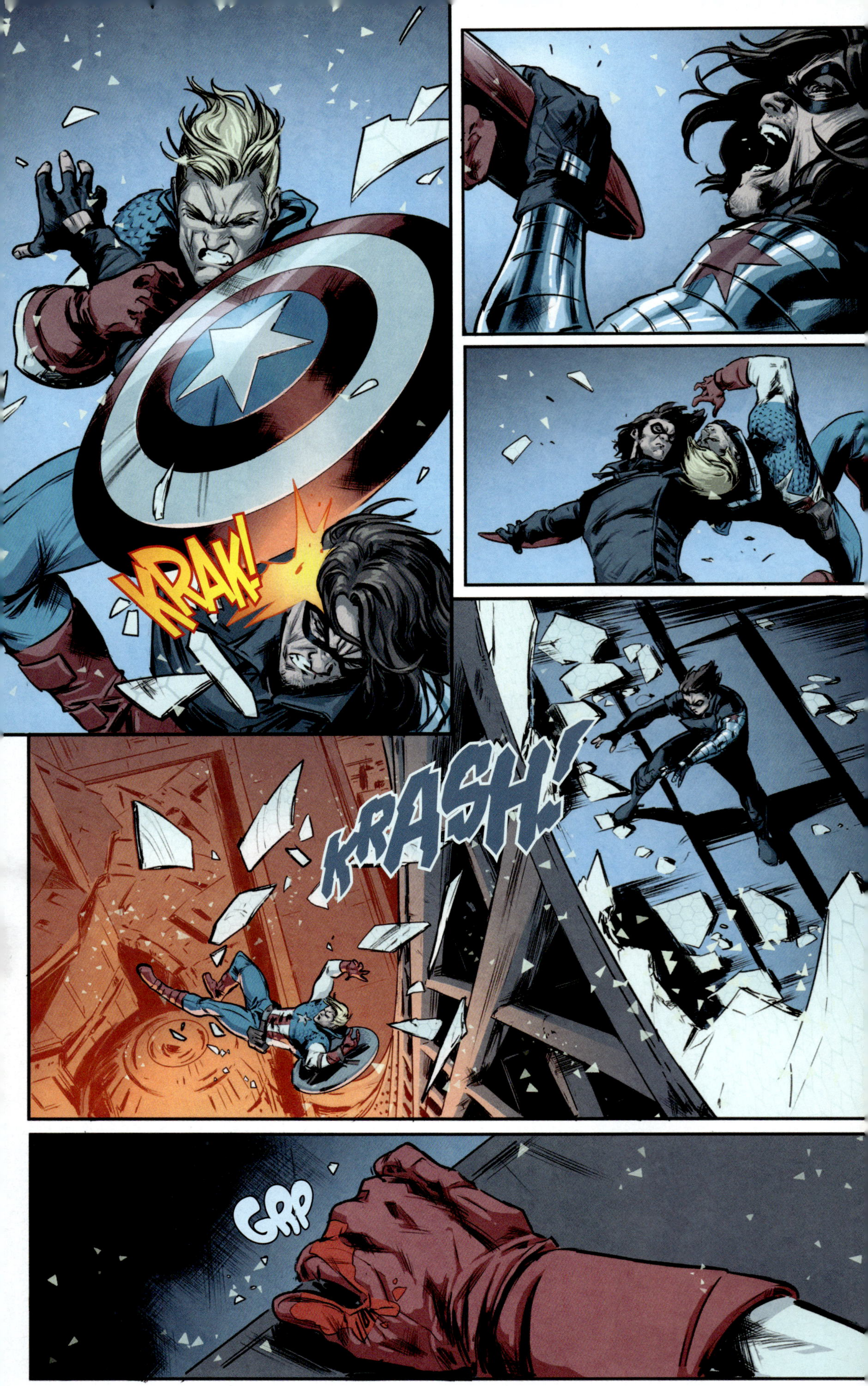
KRAK!
KRASH!
GRIP

THOOM

KRA-KOOM!

C13
C13

YOU DONE YET?
LET ME GO, STEVE.
OR I'LL MAKE YOU.
WHAM
DOOM
grrp

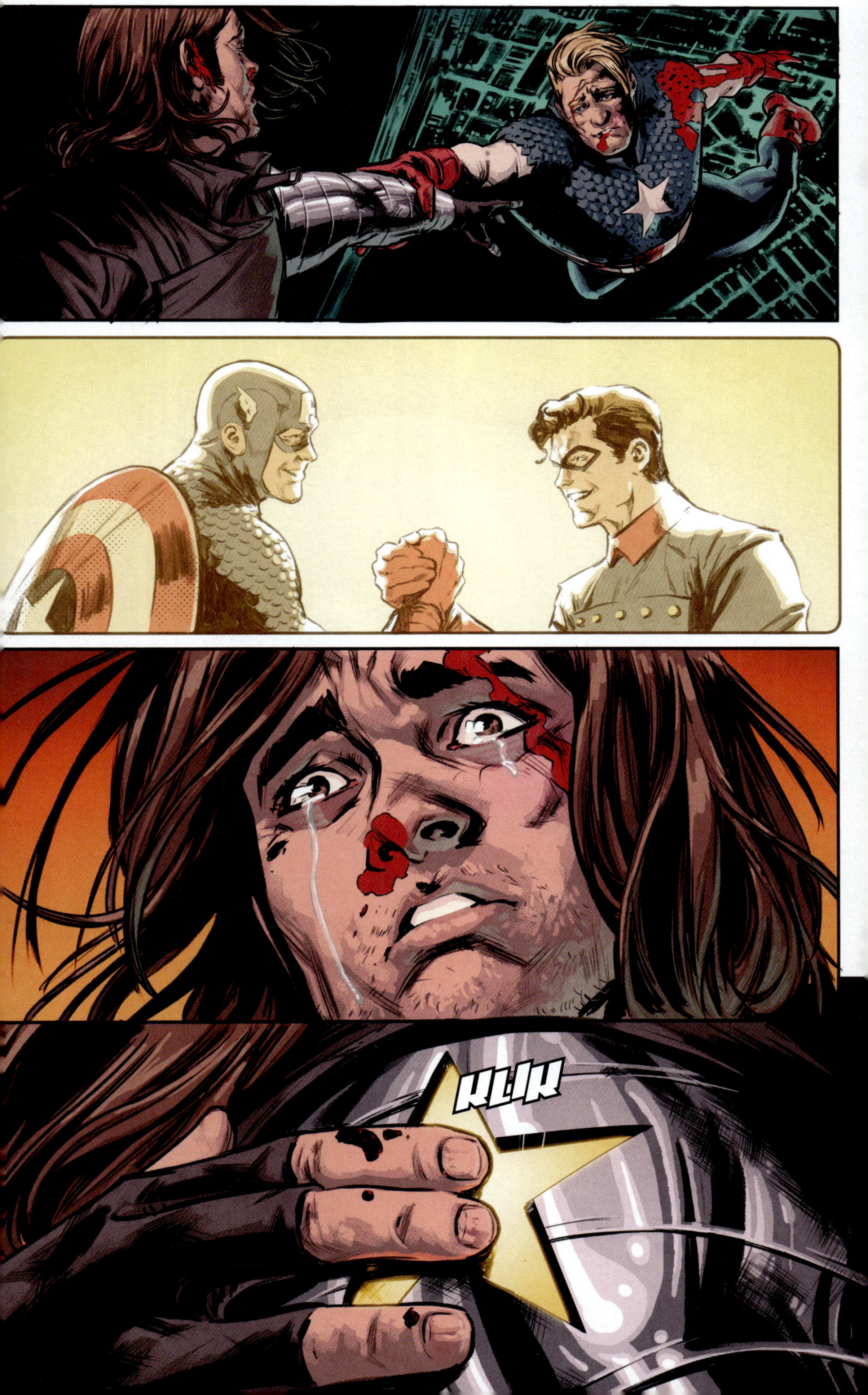
KLIK

"THE LITTLE PRUSSIAN DID IT TO US, ONE LAST TIME.

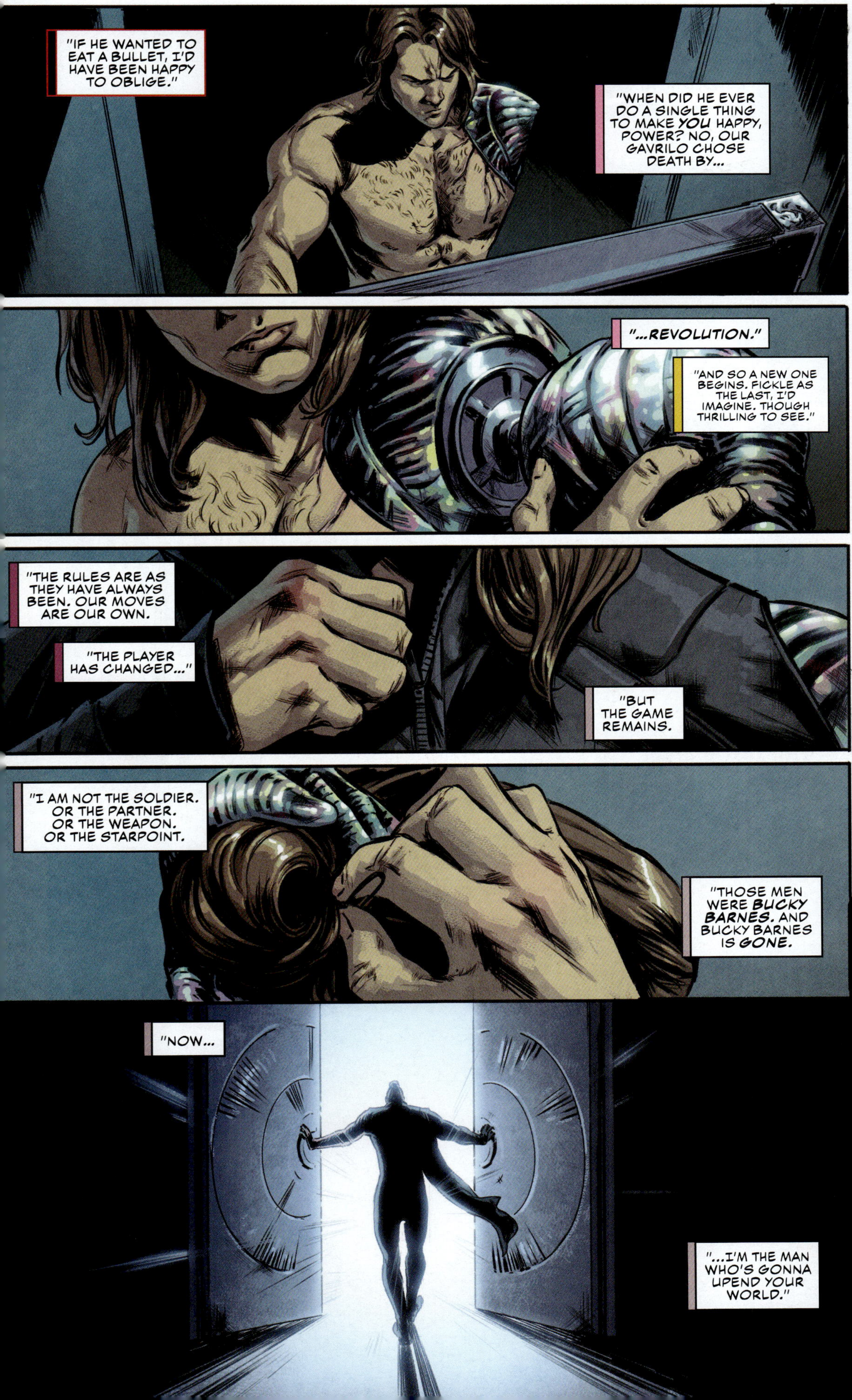
"IF HE WANTED TO EAT A BULLET, I'D HAVE BEEN HAPPY TO OBLIGE."
"WHEN DID HE EVER DO A SINGLE THING TO MAKE YOU HAPPY, POWER? NO, OUR GAVRILO CHOSE DEATH BY...
"...REVOLUTION."
"AND SO A NEW ONE BEGINS. FICKLE AS THE LAST, I'D IMAGINE. THOUGH THRILLING TO SEE."
"THE RULES ARE AS THEY HAVE ALWAYS BEEN. OUR MOVES ARE OUR OWN.
"THE PLAYER HAS CHANGED..."
"BUT THE GAME REMAINS.
"I AM NOT THE SOLDIER. OR THE PARTNER. OR THE WEAPON. OR THE STARPOINT.
"THOSE MEN WERE BUCKY BARNES. AND BUCKY BARNES IS GONE.
"NOW...
"...I'M THE MAN WHO'S GONNA UPEND YOUR WORLD."

YOU CAN CALL ME THE NEW REVOLUTION.
LET'S PLAY.
NEXT: THE INVADER!

CAPTAIN AMERICA NEEDS YOU...

TO BREAK THE OUTER CIRCLE'S CODE!

CAPTAIN AMERICA'S ENEMIES ARE ALWAYS ONE STEP AHEAD...AND NOW YOU CAN BE TOO. IT ALL STARTED WITH A KEYWORD IN **DEVIL'S REIGN: WINTER SOLDIER #1**...

THE KEYWORD UNLOCKS THE CODE, AND THE CODE UNLOCKS SECRET TRANSMISSIONS HIDDEN THROUGHOUT **CAPTAIN AMERICA: SENTINEL OF LIBERTY.** HOW DOES THE CODE WORK? WELL, WE CAN'T REVEAL ALL OUR SECRETS...BUT YOU'RE WELCOME TO TRY TO UNCOVER THEM.

THIRTEEN CODED MESSAGES HAVE BEEN PUBLISHED PRIOR TO THE RELEASE OF ISSUE #6--CAN YOU FIND AND DECRYPT THEM ALL? IF YOU THINK YOU'VE MANAGED IT, EMAIL US AT **MHEROES@MARVEL.COM** WITH YOUR EMAIL MARKED **"OKAY TO PRINT"** AND WE'LL LET YOU KNOW HOW YOU DID! BUT BE WARNED...ONE OF THEM MIGHT TAKE A **SECOND** TO FIND.

KEEP YOUR EYES OPEN, TRUE BELIEVERS. BECAUSE ONCE A CODE IS BROKEN...IT'S NOT MUCH GOOD ANYMORE, IS IT?

CODE MASTER, SIGNING OFF.

LETTER	BECOMES
J	A
I	D
M	C
B	D
A	G
R	F
N	G
E	J
S	I
C	J
D	K
F	L
G	M
H	N
K	O
L	P
O	S
P	R
Q	S
T	T
U	W
V	V
W	W
X	X
Y	A
Z	Z

SIMONE BIANCHI
CAPTAIN AMERICA: SENTINEL OF LIBERTY #3 VARIANT

MARK BAGLEY & LAURA MARTIN
CAPTAIN AMERICA: SENTINEL OF LIBERTY #4 MIRACLEMAN VARIANT

NetEase
CAPTAIN AMERICA: SENTINEL OF LIBERTY #5 GAMES VARIANT

PACO MEDINA & JESUS ABURTOV

CAPTAIN AMERICA: SENTINEL OF LIBERTY #5 CONNECTING VARIANT

NIC KLEIN

CAPTAIN AMERICA: SENTINEL OF LIBERTY #6 X-TREME VARIANT